"Come on," I said.

Jeannie nodded and I led the way, being a little less careful and going a little faster than I'd come. I could feel, almost hear, my heart thumping in my chest. Little trills of fear flashed in my stomach and along my arms and legs. I was trying to push down the panic that was washing over me. When we got to where the rowboat was, I pointed Jeannie to get in. Pearl jumped in after Jeannie. I tossed the coil of rope in and got in after it. With Jeannie in the stern and Pearl in the bow, I paddled us with my broken oar, downstream, away from the island.

I wanted to go upstream, toward home. But I couldn't, against the current, with my one broken oar. I'd have to turn us around eventually, but right now panic was chasing me. All I could think of was to get us away from Luke and his bowie knife.

OTHER BOOKS YOU MAY ENJOY

Robert B. Parker

Chasing the Bear

A YOUNG SPENSER NOVEL

SLEUTH
SPEAK
An Imprint of Penguin Group (USA) Inc.

SPEAK SLEUTH
Published by the Penguin Group
Penguin Group (USA) Inc., 345 Hudson Street, New York, New York 10014, U.S.A.
Penguin Group (Canada), 90 Eglinton Avenue East, Suite 700, Toronto, Ontario, Canada M4P 2Y3
(a division of Pearson Penguin Canada Inc.)
Penguin Books Ltd, 80 Strand, London WC2R 0RL, England
Penguin Ireland, 25 St Stephen's Green, Dublin 2, Ireland (a division of Penguin Books Ltd)
Penguin Group (Australia), 250 Camberwell Road, Camberwell, Victoria 3124, Australia
(a division of Pearson Australia Group Pty Ltd)
Penguin Books India Pvt Ltd, 11 Community Centre,
Panchsheel Park, New Delhi - 110 017, India
Penguin Group (NZ), 67 Apollo Drive, Rosedale, North Shore 0632, New Zealand
(a division of Pearson New Zealand Ltd)
Penguin Books (South Africa) (Pty) Ltd, 24 Sturdee Avenue,
Rosebank, Johannesburg 2196, South Africa

Registered Offices: Penguin Books Ltd, 80 Strand, London WC2R 0RL, England

First published in the United States of America by Philomel Books,
a division of Penguin Young Readers Group, 2009
This Sleuth edition first published by Speak, an imprint of Penguin Group (USA) Inc., 2010

1 3 5 7 9 10 8 6 4 2

THE LIBRARY OF CONGRESS HAS CATALOGED THE PHILOMEL BOOKS EDITION AS FOLLOWS:
Parker, Robert B., date.
Chasing the bear : a young Spenser novel / Robert B. Parker.
p. cm.
Summary: Spenser reflects back to when he was fourteen years old
and how he helped his best friend Jeannie when she was abducted by her abusive father.
ISBN 978-0-399-24776-7 (hc)
[1. Kidnapping—Fiction. 2. Child abuse—Fiction. 3. Friendship—Fiction. 4. Bullies—Fiction.]
I. Title.
PZ7.P2346Ch 2009 [Fic]—dc22 2008052725

Puffin Books ISBN 978-0-14-241573-3

Printed in the United States of America

Design by Katrina Damkoehler
Text set in Baskerville BT

For Joanie: The One

I was sitting with the girl of my dreams on a bench in the Boston Public Garden watching the swan boats circle the little lagoon. Tourists fed the ducks peanuts from the boats and the ducks followed them.

"It's a nice place," Susan said, "isn't it, to sit and do nothing."

"I'm not doing nothing," I said. "I'm being with you."

"Of course," she said.

The swan boats were propelled by young men and women who sat in the back of the boat and pedaled. The exact appeal of the swan boats had always escaped me, though I too felt it and had, upon occasion, gone for a ride with Susan.

We were quiet and I could feel her looking at me.

"What?" I said.

She smiled.

"I was just thinking how well I know you, and how close we are, and yet there are parts of you, parts of your life, that I know nothing about."

"Like?" I said.

"Like what you were like as a kid; it's hard to imagine you as a kid."

"Even though you have often suggested that I am still a kid, albeit overgrown?"

"That's different," Susan said.

"Oh?"

"I simply can't picture you growing up out there in East Flub-a-dub."

"Your geography has never been good," I said.

"Where was it?" Susan said.

"West Flub-a-dub," I said.

"I stand corrected," she said. "What was life like in *West* Flub-a-dub?"

"Where should I start, Doctor?"

"I know your mother died right before you were born by cesarean section. And I know you were raised by your father and your mother's two brothers."

"We had a dog too," I said.

"I think I knew that as well," Susan said. "Her name was Pearl, was it not, which is why we've named our dogs Pearl?"

"German shorthairs should be named Pearl," I said. "So what else would you like to know?"

"There must be more you can tell me than that," Susan said.

"You think?" I said.

"I think," Susan said. "Talk about yourself."

"My favorite topic," I said. "Anything special?"

"Tell me about what comes to your mind," she said. "That will sort of tell us what you think is important."

"Wow," I said. "Being in love with a shrink is not easy."

"But well worth the effort," Susan said.

"Well," I said.

Susan leaned back on the bench and waited.

Chapter 2

My father and my uncles were carpenters and shared a house. They all dated a lot, but my father never remarried, and my uncles didn't get married until I left the house. So for me growing up it was an all-male household except for a female pointer named Pearl.

Parents' Day at school was a sight. They'd come, the three of them, all over six feet, all more than two hundred pounds, all of them hard as an axe handle. They never said a word. Just sat there in the back of the room, with their arms folded. But they always came. All three.

My father boxed and so did my uncles. They'd pick up extra money boxing at county fairs and smokers. They began to teach me as soon as I could walk. And until I could take care of myself, they took care of me . . . pretty good.

Once when I was ten, I went to the store for

milk and coming home, I passed a saloon named The Dry Gulch. Couple of drunks were drinking beer on the sidewalk. They said something, and I gave them a wise guy answer, so they took my milk away and emptied it out. One of them gave me a kick in the butt and told me to get on home.

When I got home, I told my uncle Cash, who was the only one there. One of them was always there. Cash asked me if I was all right. And I said I was. He asked me if I might have been a little mouthy. I said I might have been. Cash grinned.

"I'm amazed to hear that," Cash said.

"But I didn't say anything real bad."

"Course you didn't," Cash said.

"One of them kicked me," I said.

Cash nodded.

"I'll keep that in mind," he said. "And when Patrick and your father come home, we'll straighten things out."

Chapter 3

When they got home, Cash and I told them about what happened. Patrick and my father and Cash all exchanged a look, and my father nodded.

Patrick said, "If you saw him again, could you point out the guy who kicked you?"

"Sure," I said.

"Let's go down and take a look," my father said.

So all of us, including the dog, went down to The Dry Gulch and walked in.

"Sorry, pal," the bartender said to my father. "Can't bring that dog in here."

My father said to me, "See any of the people that gave you trouble?"

I nodded.

"Which ones?" my father said.

"You hear me?" the bartender said. "No dogs."

There were six guys drinking beer together at a big round table. I pointed out two of them. My father nodded and picked me up and sat me on the bar.

"Which one kicked you?" he said.

"The one in the red plaid shirt," I said.

My father looked at Patrick.

"You want him?" my father said.

"I do," Patrick said.

"Yours," my father said.

"Mister," the bartender said. "Maybe you don't hear me. Get that dog out of here . . . and get the damn kid off the bar."

Without even looking at him, my father said, "Shut up."

Pearl sat down in front of the bar near my feet. All the men at the round table were staring at us. My two uncles walked over and leaned against the wall, near the round table. Patrick was looking at the man in the red plaid shirt.

My father walked over to the round table.

"You," he said to one of the men. "Step out here."

"What's your problem?" the man said.

"I don't have a problem," my father said, "you do, and it's me."

"That kid been crybabying about me?" the man said.

"That kid is my son," my father said. "The gentlemen leaning on the wall are his uncles. We're here to kick your ass."

The man looked at his five friends and stood up.

"Yeah?" he said.

They all stood up. My father hit the man and the fight started. Pearl and I stayed quiet, watching. Behind me, I heard the bartender calling the police.

By the time the cops arrived, both the men who had teased me were out cold on the floor. The man in the red plaid shirt was lying outside on the sidewalk. I don't quite know how that happened, except that my uncle Patrick had something to do with it. The other three guys were sitting on the floor looking woozy.

The cop in charge, a sergeant named Travers, knew my father.

"Sam," he said. "You mind telling me what you boys're doing?"

"They harassed my kid on the street, Cecil," my father said. "Stole his milk."

Travers nodded and looked at the bartender.

"I believe I been telling you, Tate," he said, "to keep the drunks inside the saloon."

"They got no call to come in here and beat up my customers," the bartender said.

"Well," Travers said. "They got *some* call. Your kid gets bothered by a couple drunks, you got some call."

He looked around the room and then at my father.

"Maybe not this much call," he said. "Probably gonna get fined, Sam."

"Worth the money," my father said.

Travers smiled.

"Known it was you three," he said, "I'd have brought more backup."

"Ain't supposed to bring no dog in here either," the bartender said. "Board of Health rule."

"We'll go hard on them 'bout that," Travers said.

My father came over and took me off the bar.

"Probably have to appear in court to pay the fine," Travers said.

"Lemme know," my father said.

He walked toward the door. Pearl and I followed him. My uncles closed in behind us.

And we left.

Chapter 4

"How come he didn't arrest you?" I said to my father when we got home.

"Known Cecil most of my life," my father said.

"But wasn't it against the law?" I said. "What you did?"

"There's legal," my father said, "and there's right. Cecil knows the difference."

"And what you did was right," I said.

"Yep. Cecil would have done it too."

"How you supposed to know that what you're doing is right?" I said.

"Ain't all that hard," my uncle Patrick said. "Most people know what's right. Sometimes they can't do it."

"Or don't want to," Cash said.

"But how do you know?" I said.

My father sat back and thought a minute.

"You can't know," he said. "But you think about it before you do it, if you got time, and then you trust yourself."

"How 'bout if you don't have time to think and you done it and it was wrong?" I said.

"Did it," my father corrected me.

He was a bear for me saying things right. Even when he didn't always say it right himself. When he wasn't around, I talked like all the other kids talked, and I think my father knew that. As long as I knew how to talk right, then I could choose.

"Sometimes you make a mistake," he said. "Everybody does."

"It sounds too hard," I said. "How do I know I can trust myself?"

"It'll be pretty much instinct," my father said. "If you been raised right."

"How do I know I'm being raised right?" I said.

My father looked at my uncles. All three of them smiled.

"None of us knows that," my father said.

I nodded. It was a lot to think about.

"How 'bout, what's right is what feels good

afterwards," my father said. "It's in a book, by a famous writer."

My father wasn't educated. Neither were my uncles. And they didn't know what they were supposed to read. So they read everything. Not long after I was born, my father bought a secondhand set of great books, bound in red leather, and he and Patrick and Cash used to take turns reading to me every night before bed. None of them had any idea what was considered appropriate for a little kid. They just took turns plowing on through the classics of Western literature in half-hour chunks every night. I didn't understand most of it, and I was bored with a lot of it. But I loved my father and my uncles, and I liked getting their full attention.

Chapter 5

"Were you scared?" Susan said. "After the fight in the barroom?"

"No," I said. "I was never scared with them."

"And you felt important to them," Susan said.

"Very."

The swan boats, escorted by ducks, moved slowly around the small lagoon, under the small bridge, around the other small lagoon, and back.

"Much of what you know," Susan said, "you learned at home."

I nodded.

"Where you felt safe."

"Sure."

"With people who loved you," Susan said.

"Absolutely."

"And they took turns," Susan said. "Reading to you and all."

"They took turns with everything," I said. "So none of them got ground down, so to speak, by being the only parent."

"And all of them trusted each other to look out for you," Susan said.

"Yes."

"Did you like the books they read to you?" Susan asked.

"I guess," I said. "Sometimes I remember something and understand it in retrospect."

"Probably better than you would if it had been taught to you in school."

"Remember the Paul Simon song?" I said.

Susan smiled and sang. Badly.

"'When I think back on all the crap I learned in high school, it's a wonder I can think at all.'"

"How come someone as perfect as you can't sing a lick?" I said.

"It's the flaw that highlights perfection," Susan said.

"Like a beauty mark," I said.

"Exactly," she said.

A squirrel darted toward us and stopped hopefully.

"Do you have anything to give him?" Susan said.

"No."

"Sorry," Susan said.

The squirrel lingered until it was clear we were a waste of time. Then he darted off.

"So it wasn't all about being tough guys," Susan said to me.

"It was never all about being tough guys," I said. "It was more about knowing what to do. They were big on knowing how to do what you needed to do. Read, fish, hunt, fight, carpenter, cook."

"Better to know than not know," Susan said.

I grinned. "They taught me about sex, quite early too."

"And well," Susan said.

Chapter 6

They'd read to me after supper.

Before supper, every other day, one of them boxed with me. They would put on the mitts and let me hammer away with one of them, my father or one of my uncles, calling out the punches.

"Left jab, jab, right cross, left jab. Jab. Jab. Left hook to the head . . . left hook to the body . . . right uppercut . . . hammer punch off the uppercut . . . right back fist."

The workout was exhausting, but it got me in shape pretty quick.

"Too many bullies in the world," Patrick used to say. "It's good to know what you're doing."

I liked the boxing. I was an energetic kid and they were all careful not to hurt me. And I liked the feeling that I might win a fight if I had one.

18

"This has got nothing to do with pushing people around," my father used to say. "This is all about a sound mind in a strong body. It's about being as complete as you can be, you know?"

I sort of knew.

Chapter 7

"And were you able to make use of your sex education?" Susan said.

"Nowhere near as soon as I wanted to," I said.

"But you had girlfriends," Susan said.

"I guess," I said. "Once I asked my father why he never got married again. 'Your mother was the one,' he told me. 'I met her early and lost her early. But I was with her for a while. I never met anyone else who was the one.'"

"But he dated a lot," Susan said.

"Sure," I said. "He liked women. He just never loved another one."

"So while you're growing up out west someplace and Susan Silverman nee Hirsch is growing up in Swampscott, Massachusetts, you're waiting to meet her?"

"Something like that."

"That's crazy," Susan said.

"I know," I said.

"But you believe it still," Susan said.

"Can't not," I said.

"Given my first marriage," Susan said, "I'd have been better off to wait for you."

Some pigeons came by to see if we were feeding anyone. We weren't and they waddled off. They should have checked with the squirrel.

"Your uncles feel deeply about her?"

"My mother? Yeah. In a different way they loved her as much as my father had."

"And you were her legacy."

"Yep."

"But you had girlfriends, before me," Susan said.

"Hell," I said. "I had to keep looking. I didn't even know your name."

Chapter 8

Jeannie Haden wasn't my girlfriend. She was a girl who was my friend. We spent a lot of time together. Things were bad at home for her. Her mother and father were getting divorced, and they fought all the time. Jeannie was scared of her father. She only went home when she had to.

"He's so mean," she used to say. "So mean."

She told me once her father had a bunch of places, "hideouts," she called them, scattered along the river, on islands. He didn't own the land. He just patched together some shacks here and there that he could go to and drink or whatever.

"He'd go there and get drunk and sometimes bring women there," Jeannie said. "I heard my mother and him fighting about it. So I snuck out and looked once. I was scared all the time. If he caught me, I don't know what he woulda done. But I had to see."

"Mighta depended on how drunk he was," I said.

"He's pretty drunk a lot," Jeannie said.

"I know," I said.

"Everybody in town knows," she said.

"I guess they do," I said.

"But they don't know about the hideouts," she said. "The one I saw was a filthy, stinky place. I don't know what kind of woman would go there."

"The kind that would go out with your pop, I guess."

"Ick," she said.

"Your mother liked him," I said. "She married him."

"She was pregnant with me," Jeannie said. "I think he was kind of handsome then."

"She must have liked him some, you know, to get pregnant," I said.

"Well, sure," Jeannie said.

"She his girlfriend at the time?" I said.

"Well, she wasn't a one-night stand, if that's what you're thinking," Jeannie said.

"I'm not thinking anything."

"My mother tries very hard," Jeannie said.

"I know she does," I said. "I didn't mean to say anything bad."

Jeannie nodded.

"I know," she said. "Poor Momma."

"She ever talk to you about it?"

"No."

"Then how do you know?" I said.

"I know when they were married," Jeannie said. "And I know when I was born."

I nodded.

"And it was him?"

Jeannie was outraged.

"You think my mother was a slut?"

"Just asking," I said. "Patrick says you don't ask questions, you don't get answers."

"The hell with him," Jeannie said.

I shrugged.

"Well, my mother wasn't sexing around, if that's what you're thinking."

"I wasn't thinking," I said. "I was just wondering. I mean, wouldn't you be glad to find out he wasn't your father?"

She started to cry.

Chapter 9

"Not what you had hoped for," Susan said.

"In those days," I said, "I knew less about why women cried."

"And now?"

"I understand why men *and* women cry," I said.

"The advantage of maturity," Susan said.

"Being young is hard," I said.

"Being grown is not so easy either," Susan said.

"But it's easier," I said.

She nodded. We were quiet for a moment.

Then Susan said, "You hunted."

"Sure," I said. "We all did."

"You don't hunt now," Susan said.

"No," I said.

"Because you disapprove?"

I shrugged.

"When we hunted, we hunted for meat," I said. "It was a way to feed ourselves. Had a vegetable garden too, and in the fall we'd preserve stuff for the winter. We were pretty self-sufficient."

Susan smiled.

"How surprising," she said.

"I liked self-sufficient," I said.

Susan smiled again, wider.

"I've always suspected that," she said.

"Are you making sport of me?" I said.

"Yes."

"I figured that right out," I said.

"I know," Susan said. "You're a detective . . . So the hunting wasn't just for fun."

"Not so much," I said. "Although it often was fun. Especially bird hunting. I liked working in the woods with the dog."

"Did you train her to hunt?" Susan said.

"No. It's probably genetic. They range like that and come back, without any training. And they'll point birds without training. But they have to be taught to hold the point. Otherwise they'll just rush in on the bird and flush it before you're ready. Before she was trained, Pearl would occasionally get one and kill it."

"Why not just let her do that? Kill them for you instead of shooting them?"

"It's harder on the bird, for one thing, and by the time you get there, the dog's got it half eaten."

Susan nodded.

"Was it ever scary?" she said.

"Pheasants rarely turn on you."

"I mean, did you ever get lost or anything?" she said.

"Me? Pathfinder?" I said. "No, I didn't. I'd been in the woods all my life. Besides, the dog always knew how to get home."

"Did you shoot anything else?" Susan said.

"Sure, antelope, elk, deer, nothing dangerous unless it fell on you."

"Never anything dangerous?" Susan said.

"Ran into a bear once," I said.

"A grizzly?"

"No, a black bear, big enough, 150 pounds maybe, bigger than I was, for sure."

Chapter 10

We were bird hunting, my father, and me, and the dog, in an old apple orchard that hadn't been farmed in maybe fifty years. You had to go through bad cover to get there: brambles and small alder that were clumped together and tangled. My father was about thirty yards off to the right, and the dog was out ahead, ranging the way they do and coming back with her tongue lolling out and her tail erect, checking in, and then swinging back out.

All of a sudden I heard the dog bark—half bark, half growl, kind of hysterical—and she came loping back, stopping and turning every few yards to make her hysterical bark/growl, and then she reached me and stood with her front legs stiff and her tail down and her ears flattened back as much as long ears can flatten. She stood there and growled and the hair along her spine stood up. Must be a hell of pheasant, I thought. And then I saw what had spooked her. It was a black bear and he had been eating the fallen apples in the abandoned orchard. The apples had probably fermented in his stomach. Because he was clearly drunk. He was standing upright, swaying a little. The dog was going crazy, growling and whining, and the bear was grunting. I had bird shot in my shotgun. It might have annoyed the bear. But it certainly wouldn't have stopped him. But I didn't have anything else, and I was pretty sure if we ran, the bear would chase us. And bears can run much faster than people. And I didn't know what the dog would do.

So I stood with my shotgun leveled, hoping that maybe, if he charged and I hit him in the face, it would make him turn. The dog was going crazy, dashing out a few feet and barking and snarling and running back to lean hard against my leg. Everything seemed to move very slowly.

And then my father was beside me. He hadn't made any noise coming. Later he told me he heard the dog and from the way she sounded, he was pretty sure it was a bear. He had a shotgun too, but it was no better than what I had. But he also had a big old .45 hog leg of a revolver that he always carried in the woods. He took it out and cocked it and we stood. The bear dropped to all fours and snorted and grunted and dipped its head and stared at us awhile. Then it turned around and left.

Chapter 11

"**My** God," Susan said. "What did your father say?"

"He said, 'Dog's no good for birds for the rest of the day and we probably ain't either.' So we went home."

"And he never said what a *brave boy* or anything?"

"He said I was smart because I'd lived to hunt another day. Then we went home and sat at the kitchen table with Patrick and Cash and I told them about what happened. Cash got up and got a bottle of scotch from the kitchen cabinet and four glasses. Then my father poured scotch in three of them and some Coke in the fourth. And we drank together."

"You'd acted like a man," Susan said. "So he treated you like a man."

"In his way," I said.

Susan smiled.

"'That brown liquor,'" she said, "'which not women, not boys and children, but only hunters drank.'"

"William Faulkner," I said.

"Very good," Susan said. "For a man with an eighteen-inch neck."

"I told you they read to me a lot."

She said it again, "'Not women, not boys and children.'"

"Sounds sort of sexist, doesn't it?" I said. "Age-ist too."

"Maybe we can have his Nobel Prize revoked," Susan said.

"Good thing was, that whenever I was in trouble, I'd think about that bear and it helped."

"Because you were brave then?" Susan said.

"I guess, although to tell you the truth, I really think more about sitting around the table drinking soda while my father and my uncles drank their scotch."

"The ritual," she said. "More than the event."

"I guess," I said. "I thought a lot about it when I was in the woods with Jeannie."

"Jeannie?" Susan said. "In the woods?"

"It wasn't what you think," I said.

Chapter 12

I was hanging outside the variety store with Pearl and some guys when Luke Haden's car pulled up at the stoplight, with Jeannie in the front seat. I had never seen her riding with her father before. She saw me through the rolled-up window and mouthed the word *HELP* at me. *HELP. HELP.* I started toward the car and the light changed and the car moved forward.

There was a trash truck behind it, much slower to move.

"Pearl," I said. "Go home."

Then I stepped up onto the back of the trash truck. There were plenty of places to stand and plenty of places to hang on. We used to ride the trucks a lot. See which of us could get the furthest before some cop spotted us and pulled the truck over and made us get off. I knew from experience that the drivers normally had the right-hand rearview mirror set wider so they could see the next lane, and, therefore, they never saw us. I stayed on the right-hand side of the truck, peering ahead at Luke Haden's car. It wasn't much of a car, a big old Ford sedan, with cardboard taped over the back where the rear window got smashed in. It had been maroon, maybe, when it was new. But what with dirt and rust and stuff it was a little hard to say what color it was now.

The car turned right, onto River Street. I knew that River Street was short, and as the truck slowed at the intersection, I jumped off and ran downhill after the car. When I got to the end, the Ford was parked on the side of the road, empty. There was a path that led to the river. I went down it, moving slower, being more careful. At the end of the muddy path was a little jetty with a couple of row-boats tied to it. I heard the sound of an outboard motor. I stepped out onto the jetty and looked. Jeannie and her father were in a bass boat with her father in back at the motor and Jeannie sitting sort of hunched up in the front.

I stared after them as they disappeared around the bend. I felt something nudge at my leg. It was

Pearl; she must have followed the trash truck and tracked me down River Street.

"Okay," I said. "I can't leave you here."

I got into one of the rowboats and gestured Pearl in after me. She sat up front, and we pushed off after them.

There was a single oar in the boat and it was broken, so I had only a short handle with a blade. It wasn't much use, but I was able to get the rowboat out into the middle of the river, where the current took over. Pretty soon, the sound of the motor faded. I used the broken oar to steer. I wasn't going to catch them at this rate, but maybe I could find where they went. Besides, I didn't know what else to do. And if I found them, then what? All I had was a jackknife. I didn't know what to do about that either. So I just drifted, following Jeannie down the big river, under the dark arch of trees that grew out from both shorelines. I felt like I was in a tunnel, without much choice about where I was going. And with no clear idea of what to do when I got there.

Chapter 13

"**How** old were you?" Susan said.

"Maybe fourteen," I said.

"Weren't you scared?"

"I was terrified," I said.

"You couldn't tell the police or your father?"

"I'd have lost them," I said. "I didn't know where they were going. I figured when they got to the river that they were going to one of his hideouts. But I didn't know where that was, not even which direction, you know? Upriver or down."

"And you had no time to think," Susan said. "And you were fourteen years old."

"Exactly," I said.

"How about the dog?" Susan said.

"She was kind of comforting, actually. She'd been on the river with me a lot over the years, and she liked riding in the boat."

"Why did you do it?" she said.

"Go after her?"

"Yes. Why didn't you say, it's an issue between a father and his child. It's not my business."

"I never thought about that," I said.

"But you were fourteen years old and alone."

"It seemed like the right thing to do," I said.

"I'm not saying it wasn't," Susan said.

"My father used to tell me, 'Every person is afraid sometimes. Thing is not to let it run you. Thing is to go ahead and do what you need to do.'"

Chapter 14

An occasional turtle splashed off a log into the water as we drifted past. In the front of the rowboat Pearl was very interested in the turtles. As she was with the frogs that jumped or the jays that flew about under the high treetops. On a small island in the middle of the river we saw a huge snapping turtle that made an odd noise, between a hiss and a grunt, at us as we floated by him. Pearl laid her long ears back flat and hunched a little at him.

She'd hunted enough and been trained enough so that she never made any noise in the woods. She'd bark at people from the front porch of our house. But in the woods she never made a sound unless we ran into a drunken bear.

Occasionally we passed a fishing camp or a little summer cottage with a boat dock. And, of course, here and there along the riverbank, with wide empty spaces in between, there were towns and roads and cars and ma-and-pa stores and people doing the stuff that people do. But on the river, mostly, we were as alone as if we had gone back in time.

White perch broke up from under water now and then to snap a dragonfly, and if I looked straight down into the rust-colored water, sometimes I'd see a channel catfish. The river smelled swampy, and along the shoreline among the trees were a tangle of wild blueberry plants and the little thorny vines that I didn't know the name of that caught at your ankles when you were hunting.

The banks of the river were muddy and the roots of trees that grew close to the river were exposed. Tree roots are not good looking. Once I saw a doe come down through the underbrush and the root tangle to drink from the river, picking her way so lightly it was like her feet were reaching down to touch the ground. Above us all, a hawk circled and banked without any effort. Once in a while he would suddenly drop like a rock into the water and fly off with a fish or a frog. He would disappear for a while and then he would be back, circling and banking effortlessly. Pearl watched him for a long time.

I wasn't wearing a watch, but the sun was very low when I spotted the bass boat. It was pulled up onto a small muddy area at the edge of a big island in the middle of the river where the river was at its wildest. The motor had been tilted into the boat, so that what I saw was the naked propeller staring out at me.

I maneuvered myself downriver, which was the only direction I could go, past the bass boat and in among the exposed roots of a cluster of birch saplings. I tied the boat to one of the saplings and sat listening. Pearl looked at me over her shoulder. What are we doing?

I put my finger to my lips, though she hadn't made any noise and I knew she wouldn't. The woods weren't quiet. There was the sound of the river and of frogs making frog sounds and birds twittering. But I heard no human sound.

I gestured to Pearl and she went out of the boat among the root tangle and up the muddy bank as lightly, almost, as the doe had come down to drink, a little ways back. I followed her. I got my feet wet and slipped once on the muddy bank, but in a minute we were both standing in a small clearing among the trees. Pearl began suddenly to sniff near the edge of some brush. Then she darted into the bushes and scrabbled around in there a minute and came out with a dead muskrat, whose neck she had just broken.

"Lucky you," I said to her. "Supper."

She showed me the muskrat. I nodded and patted her head.

"Go on," I said. "Eat it."

She looked at me and dropped the dead animal and looked at me and wagged her tail.

"Go on," I said.

She dropped her head and nosed it over onto its back and bit into its belly.

"Yum," I said.

There were some wild blueberries and I ate some while Pearl ate her muskrat. The blueberries weren't much. But they were better than raw muskrat.

Chapter 15

Luke Haden was kind of a legend among the kids, a big shambling unshaven bear of a man with lousy teeth. The town boogeyman. We were all scared of him. He had a bad reputation as a brawler, although he had always stayed clear of my father and my uncles. I never knew what he did for a living. Stole things, mostly, I think. Poached game sometimes. Odd jobs now and then.

My father said he was "a man who sucked up and bullied down." Which was probably true. But I was a kid and he scared the hell out of me.

But I needed to do what I needed to do. So when Pearl finished her muskrat, we started to ease through the woods to see what we could see. I could feel the fear in my stomach and hear it in my breathing. I smelled wood smoke and put my hand on Pearl to make sure she stayed with me.

We went toward the smoke.

In a small clearing I could see a fire. Jeannie was sitting on the ground near it, looking at nothing; some sort of lean-to shelter, made of scraps, was set up near the fire. Where was her father? I inched a little closer.

I smelled something. Something grabbed my arm. I made a little yelping noise that I hoped Jeannie didn't hear.

"What are you doing sneaking round here, boy?" Luke Haden said.

He loomed over me.

"I'm not doing nothing," I said.

The smell was booze. Not just on Luke's breath. His whole self smelled of it.

He gave me a heavy shake.

"You better say more than that, boy," he said. "Or you are in a world of trouble."

"Honest, mister," I said.

Luke slapped me across the face and everything hazed for a minute.

Beside me Pearl made a noise I'd never heard. It wasn't the hysterical barking/growling sound she'd made with the bear. This was a low growl that seemed to come out of her very center and get stronger as she growled.

"Wha's that?" Luke said, and let go of my arm and took a step back.

The minute he let go, I headed for the woods. Pearl came with me. Behind us I could hear Luke crashing into the woods. But he was fat and drunk. My haze had cleared, and Pearl and I could run like hell. In a minute or so, he gave up.

Pearl and I went to where we'd left the boat. I wanted to get in it and get off the river and run. But I couldn't. I looked at the boat. Pearl sat and waited.

"I can't run off," I said to her.

Chapter 16

"Why didn't you paddle to the riverbank and ask for help?"

"It was pretty empty country south of where I lived."

"Still, there must have been towns or a highway or something."

"Sometimes."

"So why didn't you try to get help?"

"I don't know," I said.

"Find a phone someplace and call the police?"

"I don't know."

"Call your father?" Susan said.

"I don't know."

The trees and grass muted the traffic noise outside the Public Garden. The swan boats glided. The ducks followed. We watched them for a while.

"You were a boy," Susan said.

"Yep."

"Up against not only an adult man, but a big, brutish adult male."

"Yes."

"Because Jeannie was your friend."

"Yes."

"Did you think you loved her?"

"No," I said. "I knew she wasn't the one."

"How did you know that?"

"I just knew."

Susan smiled.

"You seem not to have changed a lot since you were fourteen," Susan said.

"I'm bigger," I said.

"True."

I opened my coat.

"I have a gun," I said.

"Yes."

"And I'm with the one."

"Me too," she said.

"So, see, I have too changed," I said.

"If you were in the same situation today," Susan said, "would you go to the riverbank and call the cops?"

I looked at her. She looked at me.

"Well, now I could kick Luke Haden's butt," I said.

"You know as well as I do that you would not go ashore and ask for help," Susan said.

I shrugged.

"It has to be you," Susan said.

I shrugged again.

"Do you know why?" she said.

"Ego?" I said.

"Oh, probably some of that, but self-sufficiency comes to mind."

"Isn't that sort of like independence?" I said.

Susan smiled.

"I would guess," she said, "that independence was the result of self-sufficiency."

"Wow," I said. "You must have a PhD from Harvard, way you talk."

"Aw, it's nothing," Susan said.

"You think I was born that way?" I said. "Or did I learn it from my family?"

"Nature or nurture?" Susan said.

"Uh-huh."

"I don't know," Susan said.

"You don't know?" I said.

"Nobody else does either," Susan said.

"But you have a PhD," I said.

"From Harvard," Susan said.

"And you don't know either?" I said.

"No."

"Then it must be unknowable," I said.

"That's the only explanation," Susan said.

Chapter 17

Pearl and I slickered around the rim of the island in the rowboat, trying to come at the camp from a different side. When I thought we were about opposite where we had been, I pushed into the bank, tied the boat and we went ashore. It was jet dark in the woods and hard going. I went slow and careful and very low, pulling loose from the thorny vines, scraping myself on branches that stuck up unexpectedly from fallen trees, banging my knee at least once on a rock I didn't see. Pearl proceeded without difficulty, though I noticed that she let me break trail.

I could smell the campfire, and if I looked up, I could see the glow of it above the tree line. Finally when I figured I was opposite the place where Luke had seen me last, I got down on my stomach and wriggled closer through the brush.

They were there. Jeannie was still sitting on

the ground by the fire. Luke was sort of lying down next to her, propped up on his elbow, drinking from a big mason jar of clear moonshine whiskey. On his belt was a great big bowie knife.

"Got as much right to you as she does," he was saying. "You my flesh and blood, my own flesh and blood."

"You just want me so Mom can't have me," Jeannie said.

"See how she likes it," he said.

"Likes what?"

"See she likes it," Luke mumbled.

He was beyond drunk. I looked at the little camp. The lean-to was held up by rope between two trees. The leftover rope lay loosely at the foot of one tree. There was a lot of it. Under the lean-to I could see a blanket roll. He hadn't bothered to unroll it.

"You sure you don't know who that kid is?" Luke said.

"I don't know who he is," Jeannie said.

"He better not come round here again," Luke said.

"I want to go home," Jeannie said.

"Mind your mouth, girl. You think you too big to whup?"

"I hate you," Jeannie said.

Luke lurched toward her a little and rolled over on his face. He was too drunk to get up.

"Hell with you," he mumbled, and got himself back up on his elbow and drank some more moonshine.

"Hell with you," he said. "Hell with you . . . ."

Jeannie didn't speak. She sat with her head down. I waited. In a few minutes Luke began to snore. Jeannie paid no attention to him. I waited a little longer. The snoring persisted. I stood and walked to the edge of the lean-to. Jeannie saw me and her eyes widened. I put my finger to my lips. She didn't move. I pointed to the blanket roll and then to her and jerked my thumb toward the woods behind me. She nodded and got up quietly. He didn't stir, just lay on his side snoring, reeking of moonshine. Jeannie picked up the blanket roll and went into the woods behind the lean-to. I cut off the leftover rope with my jackknife and coiled it around my arm and hand and followed her. I didn't have a plan for the rope. I just thought it might be useful. When we were in the woods, Pearl was sniffing Jeannie and wagging her tail.

"Come on," I said.

Jeannie nodded and I led the way, being a little less careful and going a little faster than I'd come. I could feel, almost hear, my heart thumping in my chest. Little trills of fear flashed in my stomach and along my arms and legs. I was trying to push down the panic that was washing over me. When we got to where the rowboat was, I helped Jeannie get in. Pearl jumped in after Jeannie. I tossed the coil of rope in and got in after it. With Jeannie in the stern and Pearl in the bow, I paddled us with my broken oar, downstream, away from the island.

Chapter 18

I wanted to go upstream, toward home. But I couldn't, against the current, with my one broken oar. I'd have to turn us around eventually, but right now panic was chasing me. All I could think of was to get us away from Luke and his bowie knife.

We stayed in the middle of the river, riding the current. Where the treetops didn't touch, the moonlight showed through and looked really nice reflecting on the surface of the river. It was quiet as it ever gets in the woods. The soft river sound. An occasional frog grunt. Now and then a night bird. And once, I heard a fox bark. Pearl stiffened and pricked her ears and stared at the fox bark for a long time. But no fox appeared and after a while she gave up on it.

"You came after me," Jeannie said.

"Yep."

She didn't say anything. The panic was slowly draining from me as we went downriver. I felt exhausted. And hungry. And thirsty.

"What's in the blanket roll?" I said.

"Some peanut butter," Jeannie said. "And some crackers, and I think a few bottles of Coke or something. I don't know if there's anything else."

"Let's unroll it," I said. "And see."

She did. It was the way she'd described it, plus a big box of Oreo cookies. I gave her my jackknife, and she made us a bunch of cracker and peanut butter sandwiches and handed me back my knife. We each drank a Coke with the crackers.

"Where'd you get the knife?" she said.

"My father gave it to me for my eighth birthday. He said it was a handy thing to carry."

"And you've carried it ever since?"

"Yeah," I said. "Sure."

"Are you scared?" she said.

"Yes."

"Me too," she said. "You don't seem scared."

"I'm trying not to let it run me," I said.

"My father is so awful," she said.

"Yes," I said.

"When I said 'help' to you in the car, I was thinking maybe you'd get your father or one of your uncles."

"Wish I had," I said.

"Why didn't you?"

"No time," I said. "If I lost contact with you, I wouldn't have known where to look."

She nodded.

"I think you are very brave," she said.

"I'd feel braver if I wasn't so scared," I said.

"Maybe he won't follow us," Jeannie said. "Maybe he'll wake up and find me gone and say to hell with it. Or maybe he won't even remember I was with him. He forgets stuff a lot."

"Or maybe he'll come after us like a bat out of hell. My uncle Cash always says that you can hope for the best, but you need to be ready for the worst, you know?"

"Yes," she said.

I felt my eyes blink shut for a moment and my head drop. I jerked my head up and opened my eyes.

"We gotta sleep," I said.

"Okay," she said.

I worked us over to the shore with my broken oar and pulled the boat into a little cove.

"Can you carry the stuff?" I said.

Jeannie nodded and gathered the blanket roll into a kind of a sack. I bumped the rowboat against the bank. Pearl hopped out and began to sniff around. Jeannie climbed out carrying the blankets and stuff. I tied the rowboat to a bush that hung over the water. Then I climbed out and followed Pearl and Jeannie up the bank. It was dark under the trees. I could hear Pearl snuffling around in the darkness. We were in a small clearing under some high pine trees. I was so tired I could barely stand.

Jeannie took the food from the blankets. I gave Pearl some peanut butter and crackers. Then I took a blanket and gave the other one to Jeannie.

"Will you be able to sleep?" I asked.

"Maybe. What if he comes and spots the boat?" Jeannie said.

I took the rope and strung it about a foot off the ground across the area between us and the river.

"He won't see this in the dark, maybe trip on

it. Might wake us up, or at least Pearl, and maybe we can get away. Right now, I gotta sleep."

The ground was covered with pine needles. I got rid of a couple of sticks and a rock and lay down with the blanket around me. The blanket didn't smell so good. But I was too tired to care. Jeannie lay down beside me, and Pearl burrowed between us.

"My father is afraid of dogs," Jeannie said. "Always was. Says it's 'cause somebody set their dogs on him when he was a kid."

"Good," I said, and fell asleep.

Chapter 19

"Do you happen to have a jackknife on you, as we speak?" Susan said.

I grinned and took a small buck knife out of my pants pocket.

"Surprise, surprise," Susan said. "Same knife?"

"No," I said, "but same kind."

"And has it been useful?"

"Very," I said. "My father used to trim his nails with his."

"With a knife?"

"Yeah."

"Egad," Susan said.

"What's wrong with that?" I said.

"I grew up a nice Jewish girl in Swampscott, Massachusetts. I know nothing of the world of bears and buck knives."

"I've done what I can to educate you."

Susan nodded.

"And I'm grateful," she said. "So did her father show up in the night?"

"No," I said. "I slept like we used to sometimes, when we were kids. Close your eyes for a moment at night and open them a second later and it's morning."

"I remember," Susan said.

"When I opened my eyes, I was looking up through the trees and seeing blue sky. There were a few white clouds, and the birds were singing. I didn't know where I was for a minute. Pearl was sleeping beside me on her back with her feet in the air, and Jeannie was beyond her. And I sat up and looked around and remembered."

"What did you do about the bathroom?" Susan said.

I smiled.

"I was embarrassed to death thinking about it. But Jeannie just got up and said to me, 'I have to go to the bathroom,' and strolled off into the woods. I scooted off in the other direction."

"Women are generally calmer about such matters," Susan said.

"I didn't realize nice Jewish girls from Swamp-scott even went to the bathroom."

"We don't," Susan said. "But I have a lot of non-Jewish friends."

"Like me," I said.

"Especially like you," she said. "Was she cute?"

"Jeannie?"

"Mm-hmm."

"Hard to describe. I mean, she had long brown hair and even features and her skin was kind of pale and she had nice lips, sort of full. Like yours. But what I remember most about her was this kind of softness she had, gentleness maybe, but affectionate. I bet she grew up to be a passionate woman."

"Like me," Susan said.

"Well, maybe not that passionate."

"So what'd you do?" Susan said.

"We ate some Oreos for breakfast and drank a little of the Coke, and then I climbed a tree and looked around. I couldn't see anything on the river. I couldn't see anything inland except more trees. No highways, no towns. No sound of traffic, no church bells, no factory whistles, no sirens, nothing."

"And you didn't know where you were," Susan said.

"Not really. I didn't know how fast we were going on the river. So, I didn't know how far downriver we were. I could tell from where the sun came up what direction we were heading. But that aside, I hadn't a clue."

"So what did you do?"

I shrugged.

"I decided to keep going until I found a bridge, or a highway or a town or something," I said.

"Going further away from where you wanted to be."

"I didn't know what else to do," I said.

"Like your father said, you were smart. You knew when not to fight. So you got back in the boat?"

I nodded.

"Back in the boat," I said.

Chapter 20

It would have been peaceful drifting along on the river, under the trees, if there weren't somebody after us with a bowie knife. And if we had something besides Oreo cookies for breakfast.

"Do you think he's still after us?" Jeannie said.

I noticed dark bruises on her wrists. Probably from when her father grabbed her.

"Don't know that he's not," I said.

"He'll be drunk," Jeannie said.

"Still?" I said.

"He's drunk all the time," Jeannie said. "I don't think he can stand being him if he's sober."

"I wonder how he got to be that way," I said.

"I used to wonder that too," Jeannie said. "Now I don't even care. He's too awful."

"Was there ever a time he was nice?" I said.

"No."

"Poor devil," I said.

"Poor wife and daughter," Jeannie said.

"You don't like him at all," I said.

"I hate him," Jeannie said.

I had nothing to say to that.

Big drops of rain began to splat on the water, sending out wide ripples. I looked up through the leaves and the sky was dark. It got darker as I watched. And the rain came harder. Pearl didn't mind being wet. But she didn't like the feel of the raindrops hitting her. Jeannie unrolled the blankets and put one over Pearl. She offered me the second one.

"No," I said. "You."

"But what about you?" she said.

"I'm a Spenser," I said. "Tough."

She smiled and put the blanket over her head and around her shoulders.

"My hair must be a mess," she said.

"Kind of," I said.

"You didn't have to agree so quick," Jeannie said.

"But you still look good," I said.

"Ha!" Jeannie said.

The rain came harder. It was quite dark under the trees. The river meandered mostly, in big looping curves, so that ten miles on the river might be one mile as the crow flies. At the moment we were in one of the more or less straight stretches, and ahead of us I could see something through the murk. It might have been a bridge. The rain came straight down and fast. It was hard to see through it. We drifted toward whatever the something was, and when we got close enough, we saw it was a railroad bridge.

"Maybe it won't be raining so hard under the bridge," I said.

"But if it's a railroad bridge," Jeannie said, "won't it just be a trestle? You know, ties on a bridge frame?"

"Maybe there'll be some sort of solid cover at each end," I said.

"Can't be worse than this," Jeannie said.

I steered us with my broken oar toward the near end of the bridge. As we got close to it, I made out a sign. It said:

CAUTION
WATERFALL AHEAD
NO BOATS BEYOND
THIS POINT

I could feel the current quicken a little even as I was reading the sign. I steered the boat to the shore under the bridge and tied it to a sapling.

"Far as the boat's gonna take us," I said.

We were under a support arch of concrete at the near end of the bridge, and it did protect us from the rain. Pearl looked around at me as if to say, "It's about time." With the blanket draped on her head she looked like a painting of a Dutch peasant woman my father and I had looked at once in a museum in Denver.

"When the rain stops," I said, "we can climb up onto the bridge and follow the railroad tracks. Eventually they'll take us someplace."

"Soon, I hope," Jeannie said.

"Sooner or later, tracks lead someplace," I said.

We sat for a while under the bridge. But the rain kept coming. I was already soaked through. But it wasn't cold, and there was no wind. Once you get soaked, you get sort of used to it. We sat some more. Pearl sat under her blanket and looked at the river.

Then from upriver, a long way off, I heard something. I leaned forward trying to hear better.

"What?" Jeannie said.

I pointed upriver.

"Listen," I said.

We listened.

"My God," Jeannie said.

I nodded.

"It's the bass boat."

Chapter 21

"**What** do you think he will do if he catches us?" I said.

"He'll be drunk," Jeannie said. "He'll be very angry."

"So what do you think?" I said.

Jeannie looked at me for a while. Her eyes steady on mine. Her face perfectly still.

Then she said, "I think he'll kill you."

"And you?"

"I don't think he'll kill me," she said. "But he'll give me a fearful beating and drag me off to live with him God knows where."

I nodded.

"He'll probably kill Pearl too," Jeannie said.

I nodded again. It was like there wasn't much emotion in either of us. Like if we let it go, it would just roll over us and we'd be paralyzed. So, there we were sitting in our little boat on the river under the bridge in the rain, talking about being killed or kidnapped like we were planning to skip school.

Thanks to all the curves in the river, I knew he wasn't that close to us.

"Okay," I said. "Let's get up on the bridge."

"What are we going to do?"

"I am not gonna let him do any of it," I said.

"What are . . ."

"Come on," I said. "Take that bottle of Coke."

The crackers and cookies were a soggy mess in the bottom of the boat. I stuffed the jar of peanut butter in my shirt.

The three of us climbed out of the boat. Jeannie and Pearl headed up the bank. I wedged the broken oar into a space between the seat and the side of the rowboat. I draped the two soaking blankets over it. Then I took the coil of rope and put it over my shoulder and kicked the rowboat out into the river. It bobbed gently for a moment and then slid sort of sideways as the current caught it and turned it and began to drift it under the bridge.

In the narrowing distance the sound of the bass boat motor was getting a little louder. I turned and scrambled up the riverbank toward the bridge. Pearl and Jeannie were at the top.

"You and Pearl get behind the bushes over there," I said. "Pearl will probably want to come with me, but don't let her. If she causes you any trouble, give her a little peanut butter. She'll lap it off your finger."

"What are you doing?" Jeannie said.

Her voice was sounding panicky.

"Stay right here until I come back," I said.

"What?"

I shook my head and turned and ran to the center of the railroad bridge, bending as low as I could. The bass boat was closer. I looked over the edge of the bridge, and the caution sign was there, nailed to one of the bridge timbers. I lay flat and reached over and with both hands bent the bottom of the sign up toward me. It pulled loose. I dragged it up onto the bridge and laid it across the ties, with the writing facing up.

I started to get up and the bass boat came around the bend of the river. I dropped back flat again, lying against one of the big creosote-stinking timbers, trying to be invisible.

He probably wouldn't have seen me even if he looked up. The hard rain in his face would make it difficult to see. As the bass boat got closer, I could see that he was drinking from a mason jar. As he came to the bridge, he looked up. He was so close I could see him squinting against the rain.

Then he was under the bridge, and I was looking straight down at him. I was so still I'm not sure I breathed at all while he was beneath me. He was wearing a yellow slicker and a nasty-looking felt hat. I couldn't see the bowie knife, but I knew it was there, inside the coat.

When he was past the bridge, I swiveled slightly to watch. Ahead of him my rowboat with the blankets bunched in the back was drifting along in the murk. He must have seen it too, because I heard the motor on the bass boat rev a little higher. Then the rowboat drifted around the bend, and, closing on it fast, the bass boat disappeared right after. I stood and ran to the shore where Jeannie was.

"What?" she said.

"Stay there," I said.

I ran past her through the woods, toward the bend in the river. I got to the bend in time to see my rowboat go over the falls. The motor on the bass boat was screaming as Luke tried to turn and go back upstream. He couldn't. The current was too strong. It pushed the bass boat stern first to the top of the falls. Luke stood at the last moment as if he could dive into the water and swim to shore. Which he couldn't. The boat went over before he got out of it and he was gone.

Behind him on the river, bobbing in the current, was the nearly empty mason jar, which, before it went over the falls, filled with water and sank.

Chapter 22

We walked west along the railroad tracks, Pearl galloping ahead, exploring the woods, occasionally putting up a woodcock and looking at me in puzzlement when I didn't shoot it.

"You saw him," Jeannie said.

"Yes."

"He was dead?" she asked.

"Floating facedown," I said. "I watched him for five or six minutes. He banged round in the white water for a while and then floated downstream."

"Dead," Jeannie said.

"Had to be."

"Good," Jeannie said.

Pearl appeared from a clump of alder and looked at me and wagged her tail. I nodded, and she dashed off again into the woods. The rain didn't seem to bother her. And she didn't seem depressed about having a couple of Oreo cookies to eat. She seemed to be having a pretty good time.

"How do you feel?" I said.

"Glad," she said.

"Nothing else?"

"Relief," she said. "I mean, I know he was my father in a, you know, scientific way. But he was never a father. He was always just something to be scared of."

I looked at the bruises marking her wrist and nodded. We kept walking.

"He used to smack my mother around," Jeannie said. "Me too. Even after my mom threw him out and they got divorced, he used to show up drunk sometimes and try to make her . . . do stuff."

I nodded.

"She ever call the cops?" I said.

Jeannie shook her head.

"She was too embarrassed," Jeannie said.

"Too bad you didn't tell me more about it," I said.

"You're a kid, what were you going to do?" Jeannie said.

"I'da told my father," I said. "And my uncles."

"They would have done something?"

"Yes," I said.

The rain kept coming as we walked. It was kind of amazing how you adjust to stuff. We were wet through and had been wet through for so long that we didn't pay much attention to it anymore.

"When we get out of the woods," Jeannie said, "are we going to tell people what happened?"

"Not until we talk with my father and my uncles," I said.

"So what do we tell people?"

"That we got lost in the woods," I said.

"But you're going to tell your father the truth," Jeannie said.

"And my uncles. They'll know what to do."

"How do you know that?" Jeannie said.

"They always know what to do," I said.

"They do? My mom never does," Jeannie said.

Pearl had tired of the woods and was now trotting along the tracks in front of us. Jeannie put her hand on my arm, and we stopped for a moment. She looked straight at me.

"You saved me," she said.

I nodded.

"You knew what to do," she said.

"Didn't have a bunch of choices," I said.

In front of us, Pearl stopped suddenly and raised her head and began to sniff the air. I walked to where she stood and sniffed. There was a smell. I sniffed some more.

Someone was frying bacon. I heard a car horn. The three of us went on down the tracks, around a curve, and there was a town.

Chapter 23

"What did your father say?" Susan asked me.

"Actually it was my uncle Cash that came to get us," I said. "We were about twenty miles downriver, and we told him what happened on the ride home."

"And what did Uncle Cash say?"

"Not much. He never had all that much to say anyway."

"Did he say anything?"

"He said, 'Sounds like you done pretty good. We'll talk with your father about it.'"

"Your father was the man?" Susan said.

"It was mostly like a house with four equals in it," I said.

"Including you."

"Yeah," I said, "but in retrospect, I guess my father was a little more equal."

"And you?" Susan said.

"Maybe a little less, until I was older."

"They must have been out of their minds with worry," Susan said.

"Probably, though I gotta say they didn't mention it."

"So what was your father's reaction when you got home?"

"Mostly like Cash's, Patrick too. They both said it sounded like I'd done what I had to do and done it well."

"That must have made you feel good."

I nodded.

"Did," I said.

"How about Jeannie?"

"My uncle Cash told her that she could think of us as family and anytime she needed help come to one of us. Patrick and my father said that was so."

"And?" Susan said.

"And she started to cry."

Susan nodded.

"Finally," she said, "someone to depend on. Must have felt good for her."

A couple of pigeons came to where we sat on the bench and stood giving us the beady eye. We had no food to give them. So after a long accusatory moment, they waddled to the next bench.

"Did you know," Susan said, "in certain tribal cultures of the early Middle Ages, the child of a princess was raised by her brothers?"

"I didn't know that," I said. "Why did they do that?"

"Something about keeping the question of bloodline in-house, so to speak," Susan said.

"A little-known fact," I said.

"I have a PhD from Harvard," Susan said. "I know many of them."

"All of them as useful as that?" I said.

"Oh, heavens no," Susan said. "But I do have a question."

"Of course you do," I said. "You're a shrink."

"How did you feel?" she said.

"Me?"

"You. You were fourteen years old and you'd just killed a man."

"At the time, I didn't know quite how I felt," I said. "I'm not sure I do now."

Chapter 24

Cash drove Jeannie home. I took a shower and put on clean clothes. There were biscuits left over from breakfast. My father cooked up some antelope steaks and fried some green tomatoes. When Cash came back, we sat down to supper at the kitchen table.

"She got her story straight?" my father said.

"Yeah," Cash said. "Tell it just like it happened until the bridge. They hid on the bridge, he went on past them downriver. Don't know where he is."

"Work for you?" Patrick said to me.

I nodded.

I said, "I did kill him, though, didn't I?"

Patrick and Cash both looked at my father.

"You made it easier for him to kill himself," my father said. "But you didn't make him kidnap Jeannie, or beat her, and you didn't make him chase you down the river with a bowie knife. And you didn't require him to do it drunk, understand?"

"So why not just tell the whole truth?"

"It saves some trouble if we don't," my father said. "I told you once that there was right and wrong and there was also the law. Law can't always be about right and wrong. Sometimes the law gotta do what the law is required to do. I know and you know and Patrick knows and Cash knows and Jeannie knows that what you done was not only right, it was . . ."

He mulled his word choice for a minute.

"It was goddamned heroic," he said. "But the law can't just know things. It has to decide them in a legal way. They got to investigate. They got to talk about it in the DA's office. Maybe they have to talk about it in court. Things drag on. They finally decide that what you done was self-defense, and they leave you be. And we're right where we are now. Except in the meantime we all been annoyed at some length."

"Why does it have to be that way?" I said.

"'Cause not everybody agrees on what's right," Cash said.

"Luke Haden probably thought he was right," Patrick said. "If he cared."

"So a . . . country, a state, whatever, gotta have laws to protect us from the people who don't know what's right or don't care," my father said.

We all ate in silence for a while.

"Course that's what I think," my father said. "But you got a right to think different. If you think you need to tell the law everything that happened, and I can't talk you out of it, then I'll go down to the station with you and go the whole way with you, whatever way it goes."

I looked at my uncles.

"A course," Cash said.

"Naturally," Patrick said.

"But you all think it would be a mistake," I said.

"Never a mistake," Patrick said, "to do what you think is the right thing to do."

My father nodded.

Cash said, "Amen."

"So how can you be sure what you think is right, is right?" I said.

"I don't know," my father said.

"So what do I do?" I said.

My father grinned.

"Best you can," he said.

"I think I got to tell the truth," I said.

My father nodded.

"Okay," he said. "We'll go down tomorrow, talk to Cecil. All of us."

Chapter 25

In the morning my father drove me down to the police station and waited for me outside in the car while I went in to see Cecil Travers.

The policeman at the desk told me to sit down and Sergeant Travers would come out for me.

I sat on the hard oak bench near the station house door and in maybe five minutes Cecil Travers came out.

"Come on into my office," he said. "Tell me what I can do for you."

Cecil listened very carefully to everything I said. And nodded and listened and nodded and listened. When I got through, he leaned back in his chair and looked at me.

"You're a smart kid," he said.

And I shrugged.

"Brave too," he said.

"I was scared all the time," I said.

"Had reason to be," Cecil said. Then he cleared his throat. "I don't see enough evidence here to charge you with a crime."

"Even though I moved the sign?"

"That is correct," Cecil said.

"He might not have died if he'd been able to see the sign," I said.

"But you might have," Cecil said. "And what about the girl?"

I nodded.

"You're a kid," Cecil said. "You did the best any kid could do, with what you had, and you won. Take it and go home and be proud of it. Hell, nobody's even reported Luke missing."

"Poor guy," I said.

"Poor guy would have cut you up if he'd caught you," Cecil said.

I nodded.

"Nobody even knows he's gone," I said.

Cecil stood and came around his desk.

"And nobody cares," Cecil said. "Your old man outside?"

"Yeah."

"I'll walk you out," Cecil said.

We went through the station house and down the wide granite steps to where my father was parked in a no-parking zone, waiting for me to come out.

"Not enough of a case here for me to press charges," Cecil said.

"Good," my father said.

I got in the front seat beside him.

"Sam," Cecil said.

"Yeah?"

"You boys done a darn good job with this kid," he said.

"I think he's done most of the good work," my father said. "Me and Cash and Patrick mostly just stayed out of his way."

"Well," Cecil said. "You got reason to be proud of him."

"We are," my father said.

I was trying to stay dignified. Cecil put his hand through the open window and shook my hand. Then he turned and walked back into the station. We pulled away from the curb.

"How you feeling?" my father said.

"Pretty good," I said.

Chapter 26

"Why do you suppose you did that?" Susan asked.

"Should I lie back on this bench, Dr. Silverman?"

"Professional reflex, I suppose," Susan said. "On the other hand, my interest in you is not entirely professional."

"I've noticed that," I said.

"I love you and I want to know about you," she said.

"Anything in particular?" I said.

"Everything," she said. "And now that I have you rolling, it's hard not to keep pushing."

"I read someplace that wanting to know everything about a person is wanting to possess them."

"I believe that is probably true," Susan said.

"You want to possess me?" I said.

"Entirely," Susan said.

"Isn't that dangerous for my ego?" I said.

Susan smiled.

"If I may say so, your ego is entirely impregnable."

"Only child of a loving family," I said.

"Buttressed by accomplishment," Susan said.

"My father and my uncles were pretty impregnable too," I said.

"And to grow up," Susan said, "sooner or later, you had to separate from them."

"You think that's what I was doing?"

"When you went to the police?" Susan said. "Yes."

As one of the swan boats made its leisurely turn in front of us, a little boy was leaning out, trying to trail his hand in the water. His mother took hold of the back of his shirt and hauled him back in.

"Why then?" I said.

Susan waited. I thought about it.

"Because I had just done an adult thing," I said, answering my own question. "And I needed to what? Confirm it?"

"What happened when you had that trouble, with the men from the barroom?" Susan said.

"My father and my uncles came down and . . . fixed it," I said.

"And the bear?"

I nodded.

"My father came along and fixed it," I said.

"And the business on the river?"

"I fixed it," I said.

Susan nodded.

"And I had to fix it all the way," I said. "I couldn't let them fix the cover-up, so to speak."

"Correct," Susan said.

"It would have been a step back into childhood," I said.

"Yes," Susan said.

We were quiet. The light on Boylston Street turned green behind us and the traffic moved forward.

"You know a lot of stuff," I said.

"I do," Susan said. "Tell me how Jeannie was."

Chapter 27

It was late afternoon and starting to get dark. We were playing basketball, half-court, three on three, outdoors behind the junior high. There was a bench alongside the court and Jeannie Haden sat by herself on it watching us play.

When we got through, I walked over to her.

"You win?" she said.

"Jeannie," I said. "You been watching us play since school got out. Don't you keep track of the score?"

"I was just watching you," she said.

"Oh."

"Want to walk me home?" she said.

"Sure," I said.

"Want to stop on the way and buy me a Coke?" she said.

"Sure," I said.

We walked along Main Street to Martin's

Variety, which sold bread and milk and canned foods and had a lunch counter down one side of the store. Most of their earnings probably came from the lunch counter, because the kids had pretty well taken over the store as a hangout, which meant that generally nobody else came in.

Jeannie and I said hello to some other kids as we walked down the counter and found two seats at the end where it curved.

A guy named Croy said to me, "Hey, Spenser the river rat."

"Just as smart," I said. "But not as good looking."

Croy gave it a big haw and elbowed one of his friends. He was a year older than I was, a big kid, fat mostly, but big enough to bully the younger kids.

We sat. Jeannie ordered a Coke. I had coffee.

"You don't like Coke anymore?" Jeannie said.

"Like coffee better," I said.

She nodded.

"Lotta kids know about us on the river," she said.

"They got the story straight?" I said.

"Mostly," Jeannie said. "Nobody seems to know about you moving the sign."

"Good," I said.

Croy yelled down the counter at me.

"How about Jeannie the Queenie," he said. "Have any fun with her in the woods?"

"You shut your mouth, Croy," Jeannie said.

"Bet you did," Croy said. "She hot, Spenser?"

I looked at him silently, the way I'd seen my father do when people annoyed him.

"No sense shouting back and forth," my father used to say. "If it's not worth fighting about, then it's not worth a lot of mouth. If it is worth fighting over, then you may as well get straight to it."

So far it wasn't worth fighting about.

But it was close.

"Look at that, Barry," Croy said to his friend. "Spenser the river hero is giving me a cold stare. Hot damn, is that scary or what?"

Barry was not a threat. He was a tough guy by association, hanging around with Croy probably made him feel important. He nodded.

"Scary," he said.

"I'm betting it's 'cause he don't know what

to say, 'cause they did it and he don't want to admit it."

"I'm betting that too," Barry said.

"He do it to you, Jeannie Queenie?"

I stood up.

"I'll be back," I said.

Jeannie's face had an odd flush to it. I walked down to where Croy was sitting and jerked my head at the door.

"What?" Croy said. "You want to go outside?"

I nodded and kept walking toward the door.

"You little twerp," Croy said. "You want to fight me?"

"Yep," I said, and went out the front door and walked down the three steps and turned and waited. In a minute Croy pushed the door open. His face looked a little tight. He was mostly mouth and probably deep down he knew it.

"You sure you want to do this, kid?" Croy said.

"Yep."

"I don't want to hurt you," Croy said.

I put my hands up, like I did every weekday evening with my father and my uncles and had done every weekday evening with my father and my uncles since I was six.

"Good," I said. "But I want to hurt you."

He didn't like the boxing stance. But he was too far into this to back out. People had crowded out of Martin's to watch. He was stuck. He came down the step and walked at me.

I stuck a left jab onto his nose to stop him. It did stop him and it made his nose bleed. He shook his head and swung at me with his right hand. I blocked the punch and hit him with a straight right on his nose again. This time I broke it.

He yowled and took a step back and covered his face with his hands. Then he took his hands away a little and saw the blood and stared at it. Then he stared for a moment at me. Then he turned and pushed through the people watching and went away, walking very fast.

"Wow," Barry said. "You can really fight."

I dropped my hands and nodded to him.

"Keep it in mind," I said.

And went back into Martin's.

Chapter 28

I walked Jeannie home later that night. When we got to her house, we stopped and she turned and faced me.

"You're always taking care of me," she said.

"Not always," I said.

"I'm serious," she said. "You took care of me on the river. You defended me from Croy."

She seemed kind of intense. I didn't know what to say. I was a little uncomfortable.

"You like me," she said. "Don't you?"

"Sure," I said. "I known you since first grade."

She stood close to me, looking at me. I realized I was supposed to do something.

"I mean, you really like me," she said.

"I do," I said.

She sort of lunged forward and put her arms around me and raised her face. I realized I was supposed to kiss her. So far in life, I'd had more fights than kisses. She pressed herself hard against me. A feeling of, like, overheating flashed through me. I felt a little short of breath.

"Show me how much you like me," she whispered. "Kiss me."

I stared down at her face. Her eyes were closed. I realized I didn't quite know what I should do. Some of the women my father and my uncles brought home had kissed me on the cheek. I knew I shouldn't kiss her on the cheek. Okay, I thought, and took in a breath and bent down a little and kissed her on the mouth. She kissed back hard with her lips tight together. It hurt a little where the inside of my lip was pressed against my teeth.

I felt more of the overheating feeling. But not much else. No stars fell. No skyrockets. No moonbeams. No music. She kept pressing against me. I didn't think this was going the way it should. I liked her fine, but not the way I think she wanted me to. And I thought we might be making a mistake that we weren't really ready to make. On the other hand, there was that overheated feeling and the sense that I didn't want to hurt her feelings.

She broke off her kissing and leaned back with her arms still around my waist and looked up at me.

"My mom doesn't come home until eleven," she said. "You want to come in?"

From off to one side, where there was the me that always looked on calmly, I heard myself say, "Sure."

My voice sounded kind of hoarse, I thought.

Chapter 29

"No surprise there," Susan said. "A young woman with an abusive absentee father whose mother feels a woman is incomplete without a man."

"I was a little surprised at the time," I said.

"You were fourteen," Susan said.

"I was," I said.

The sun was now entirely behind the low buildings in the Back Bay, and the people walking past us in the Public Garden looked like people going home from work.

"So here she is kidnapped by her brute of a father and the handsome young Galahad comes galloping"—Susan smiled—"or in this case, mostly drifting downriver and saves her."

"My strength was as the strength of ten," I said. "Because my heart was pure."

"Sure it was," Susan said. "And then you defend her honor from a local bully."

"It was probably mostly about my own honor," I said.

"Probably," Susan said. "But she almost had to fall in love with you."

"Or what she thought was love."

"Shrinks call it cathexis," Susan said.

"Cathexis?"

"A powerful emotional investment in something or someone, which in fourteen-year-old girl terms feels like love, but probably isn't."

"You were once a fourteen-year-old girl," I said. "Did you do a lot of cathexis?"

"Several times a year," Susan said. "But I was, of course, always waiting for the one."

"Are you making sport of my obsession?" I said.

"I am," Susan said. "How did it work out after that night?"

"Not too well," I said. "She always sat beside me in study hall. She wanted to hold my hand if we walked anyplace. She started talking all the time about *us*."

"And that wasn't what you wanted."

"No. She was a friend, but not the only one.

Sometimes I wanted to play ball or hang with the guys."

"Did you tell her this?" Susan said.

"Yes."

"How did you break it to her?" Susan said.

"I told her about what I just told you," I said. "That she was a friend, but not my only friend. And, you know, we didn't have an exclusive contract."

"How did she take it?"

"She cried," I said.

Susan nodded.

"I remember so clearly. It was raining like hell, and a lot of wind, and we were standing under the marquee of the Main Street Movie Theater to stay dry. She cried for a little bit, and I felt I had to put my arm round her shoulders, at least. And she shook it off, and took in a big deep breath, and said, 'No. I'm okay.' And I said, 'You're sure?' and she said, 'I can wait.' And I didn't say anything. And she said, 'But I have to walk. You have to walk with me.' And I said, 'Okay.' And we walked for about an hour in a driving rain. And when we finally went to her house, she turned around and put her head against my chest and said, 'It's okay.

I'll be fine. But I'm not giving up.' Then she gave me a little kiss on the lips and went into her house."

"How was it next day?" Susan said.

"Fine," I said. "She stayed my friend. I'm sure she was waiting to be more. But she never pressed it again."

"Good for her," Susan said.

"Good for both of us."

Chapter 30

I was in study hall pretending to take notes on a book I was reading. The book was a novel about Nero Wolfe and Archie Goodman, by Rex Stout. My father had come across a Nero Wolfe novel at the library a while ago and brought it home and we all read it, and now all of us were reading all the Rex Stout we could find. Their household was all men, like ours.

Jeannie came into the study hall and sat down beside me. The teacher eyed her, and Jeannie opened a geography book and began to look at it.

The teacher looked away and Jeannie whispered to me from behind the geography book.

"My mom wants you to come for supper," she said.

The teacher looked back at us. Her name was Miss Harris and she was lean and kind of leathery and hard eyed. She frowned and shook her head.

We were quiet. Miss Harris went back to correcting papers. The room reeked of silence.

"Sure," I whispered.

Jeannie nodded.

Miss Harris had her head down, making notes in the margin of a blue book. I could see the thin white line of her scalp down the middle of her head where she parted her hair and pulled it back tight.

"Friday night?" Jeannie whispered.

Miss Harris's head jerked up and her eyes darted around the room.

"This is a time set aside for you to study," she said loudly. "Obviously some of you think it's gossip time. You are wrong, and if you continue, you will be here late after school."

I was industriously taking notes on my Nero Wolfe novel. Jeannie appeared entranced with her geography book.

Me? Dinner with Mrs. Haden? And Jeannie?

An eraser came sailing past me from the back corner of the room and bounced off the back of a chubby girl with a hair ribbon, who was sitting right in front of Miss Harris.

"Ow," the girl said.

Miss Harris got to her feet.

"What is your problem, Betsey?" she said.

"Someone threw an eraser at me."

"Sure," I whispered to Jeannie.

She smiled and nodded.

"Do you know who threw it?" Miss Harris said.

"Joey Visco," Betsey said.

"Mr. Visco," Miss Harris said.

Joey Visco said, "Miss Harris, I didn't throw nothing."

"I didn't throw *anything*," Miss Harris said.

"I know it," Joey said.

There was a lot of giggling.

"See me after class, Mr. Visco," Miss Harris said.

"But I didn't do nothing."

"After class," Miss Harris said, and went and rested her hips on her desk and folded her arms and stared at us silently.

Chapter 31

It was a pretty bad neighborhood. Mean-looking dogs behind chain-link fences. Chickens in some of the yards. Streetlights few and far apart. I wasn't comfortable. But I figured if Jeannie could live there, I could walk through it.

I didn't want to go to dinner at Jeannie's house. But her mother had invited me, and I couldn't just say no, so here I was.

Mrs. Haden met me at the door and I put out my hand like a well-brought-up boy. She took it and then pulled me to her and gave me a hug. I had very little experience at being hugged by a woman. She was wearing a lot of perfume.

"Oh, you dear thing," she said. "Jeannie's told me so much about you."

I nodded.

"And you're so handsome too," Mrs. Haden said.

I sort of nodded and sort of shrugged.

"I just had to meet you and thank you for saving my little girl," she said.

I didn't know what to say, so I nodded again and smiled as hard as I could.

"Come in, sit down, would you like a Coca-Cola? Jeannie, get him something while I look in the oven."

"Want a Coke?" Jeannie said.

"Okay," I said.

She and her mother both went to the kitchen. They looked sort of alike. Except Mrs. Haden was about twenty years older than Jeannie and looked like she might have had a hard life. She was still kind of pretty. Her hair was long. She was slim, and she wore a lot of makeup. She had on a black dress with no sleeves and black high-heeled shoes. It seemed very fashionable to me, and I wondered why she dressed up for dinner with her daughter and a fourteen-year-old kid.

Jeannie and I drank our Coke uneasily in the living room. Jeannie's house wasn't much. I'd been there once before with Jeannie when her mother was at work. The house was shaped sort of

like a railroad car. There was a little front porch.
Then you went in the front door into the living
room, through the living room to the kitchen,
through the kitchen to a bedroom, and in a little
L off that bedroom there was a bath and another
bedroom.

Mrs. Haden had cooked a chicken and some
white rice and some frozen peas. We sat at the
kitchen table. There was a candle lit on the table.
Mrs. Haden was drinking some pink wine. "I'm
sorry I can't offer you some," Mrs. Haden said.
"But I couldn't without your father's permission."

"That's okay, ma'am," I said. "I don't enjoy
wine so much."

Actually I didn't know if I enjoyed wine or not.
I wasn't sure I'd ever had any.

"Oh, you will," she said, and drank some from
her glass.

"Yes, ma'am," I said.

"Jeannie says you don't have a mother," Mrs.
Haden said.

I ate some chicken. It was kind of dry.

"Yes, ma'am."

"You live with your father?" she said.

"And my two uncles," I said.

"Isn't that interesting," she said. "Three brothers raising a child."

"Actually they are my mother's brothers," I said. "My father and them were friends and when my mother died, they moved in to help out."

"Do you remember your mother?"

"No, ma'am."

"Three men and a boy and no women," she said.

She drank the rest of the wine in her glass.

"Oh, there's women," I said. "My father and my uncles all have a bunch of girlfriends, but none of them has got married."

Mrs. Haden gave herself some more wine.

"A house full of boys," she said.

"I guess so."

"Probably living on peanut butter sandwiches and cold beans from the can," Mrs. Haden said.

"We take turns cooking," I said.

"You too?"

"Yes, ma'am."

"Do you suppose they'd like to come here with you next time for a home-cooked meal?" Mrs. Haden said.

"I guess so," I said.

"Well, that's what I'm going to do," she said. "I'm going to invite them for a home-cooked meal."

I looked at Jeannie. She smiled blankly. I nodded.

"That would be nice," I said.

Chapter 32

Susan and I left the bench and walked up to the little bridge over the swan boat lake. We stood leaning our forearms on the railing and watched the boats and the people and the ducks, green and quiet in the middle of the city.

"It sounds like Jeannie's mother might have wanted to promote you as her daughter's boyfriend," Susan said.

"I think that was one thing she wanted," I said.

"And the other?"

"I was a way to three eligible bachelors," I said.

"Two for one," Susan said. "A boyfriend for her daughter and one for her. She seems in retrospect a woman who needed a man, who thought all women needed a man."

"She stayed a long time with one of the worst men in the world," I said.

"To some, a bad man is better than no man," Susan said. "I stayed a long time with the wrong husband."

"I think you've changed since then," I said.

"Yes, I think so," Susan said. "Did your father and your uncles go for dinner?"

"They did," I said.

"What was that like?"

"They went the way they went to PTA meetings and stuff," I said. "They didn't want to go. They didn't expect to enjoy it. They didn't enjoy it. But they were polite about it."

"Did she flirt with them?"

"Oh, my, yes," I said.

"Was it embarrassing?"

"Yes. It didn't seem to embarrass my father or my uncles, but it embarrassed the hell out of me and Jeannie."

"She get drunk?"

"Yes."

"Any of them ever ask her out?"

"No."

"They say why?"

"No."

"You have a theory?"

"She drank too much. And she wasn't very bright. And she was needy. My father and my uncles never much admired needy."

"So they just came to dinner to help you out," Susan said.

"Yes, and I suspect that if they thought I needed more help, one of them would have dated her. Probably Patrick."

"Why Patrick?"

"He was the youngest," I said. "My father asked me about my feelings for Jeannie. I said I liked her but not as a girlfriend."

"Waiting for the one?"

"I was," I said. "And she wasn't it."

"But you might well have been it for Jeannie," Susan said. "Girl with no stability at home, looking for someone, seeing it in you."

"I was fourteen," I said.

"And she probably hoped for the stability that your father and your uncles provided you, though I'm sure she didn't know it."

"She probably did, and I tried to help her with that. But she wasn't the one."

Susan smiled at me.

"What if I'd still been married when you met me?"

"I'd have made my bid anyway," I said.

"And if I hadn't responded?"

"I'd have waited awhile and tried again."

"You've never been a quitter," she said.

"No," I said.

We looked down as a swan boat slid under the bridge. A couple of kids in the front waved at us.

"I would have responded," Susan said.

Chapter 33

We played six-man football in my junior high school. I played in the three-man backfield. Since the man who received the snap from center could not run the ball past the line of scrimmage, I played sometimes at the tailback position to pass and sometimes at left halfback to take a handoff and run. The high school coach had already been to see me about next year to be sure I didn't go to St. Mary's. And everybody said I was pretty good. Which I was.

There was a dance in the school cafeteria after the last game, the week before Thanksgiving, and I took Jeannie. Even though she wasn't exactly my girlfriend. There was cider and doughnuts and some pumpkins and some big paper turkeys and music on the speaker system. We danced a little. I didn't really know how to dance. Neither did she. In fact, neither did anyone else in the room. Most of the boys were interested in dancing close. Most of the girls were trying not to get stepped on. Everyone bumped into each other a lot. Standing around the rim, several teachers watched us carefully to make sure fun didn't break out in some unacceptable way.

"Do you know any Mexicans?" Jeannie said to me.

"Mexicans?" I said. "You mean in Mexico?"

"No," Jeannie said. "Around here."

"Yeah, sure," I said. "Guy named Alex Rios, he's a mason, works with us on a lot of jobs."

"Us?"

"You know, I work with my father and my uncles in the summer," I said. "And a lot of weekends during school. One summer they weren't building anything, so I worked a couple months with a landscaping company run by Mr. Felice. Roberto Felice. All the workers but me were Mexican."

"So you don't hate Mexicans," Jeannie said.

"Like everybody else," I said. "Like some, don't like others."

"My father hated all Mexicans," she said.

"Your father probably hated all everything," I said.

We bumped and stumbled our way around the dance floor again.

"Why you asking me about Mexicans?" I said.

The music stopped, so we got some doughnuts and some cider and went and sat on a couple of folding chairs.

"We never had any money," Jeannie said. "We always lived in poor neighborhoods."

"Your old man never worked," I said.

"That's right," Jeannie said. "So my mom had to work. She was a cocktail waitress at the country club, and it meant she had to work nights."

"So who took care of you?"

"Mrs. Lopez," Jeannie said.

I nodded.

"She lived next door," Jeannie said. "And she had a little boy, about my age. Aurelio."

"Aurelio Lopez," I said.

"You know him?"

"I see him around school," I said.

"Mrs. Lopez's husband is a busboy at the club,

and he had to work nights too, so I would stay with Mrs. Lopez every night."

"How was that?"

"She was great. She is great. She's like . . ."

Jeannie stopped and took a little breath.

"I love her," she said.

"That's nice," I said.

"She's like my other mom," Jeannie said.

"Maybe that's why you turned out so good," I said.

Jeannie nodded.

"You don't like my mom," she said.

"I didn't say that."

"But you don't," Jeannie said. "I know. Lotta people don't like her. She drinks a lot . . . and she's man crazy. I bet your father doesn't like her. Or your uncles."

I shrugged.

"She's had a hard life," Jeannie said. "But she's my mom and I love her too."

"Good," I said.

One of the teachers announced over the sound system that this was the last dance. And to be sure when we left to take all of our stuff with us. No one would be permitted back in the school. And anyone who left anything would have to reclaim it at the principal's office in the morning.

Most of the kids danced the last dance. But we didn't. Jeannie wasn't finished talking.

She said, "Aunt Octavia, that's what I call her, told me a bunch of kids beat Aurelio up."

"What for?"

"For being Mexican," she said. "Said they called him names, you know, greaser, spick."

"That's lousy," I said.

"Mr. Lopez says he finds out who did it, he's gonna kill him."

"You know Mr. Lopez?" I said.

"A little," Jeannie said. "He works all the time. Aunt Octavia says he's crazy mad. And she says a lot of Mexican kids are getting beat up like Aurelio."

"For being Mexican?" I said.

"Yes."

"Lopez seems like a nice enough kid," I said.

"He is. He's not a jock or a tough guy or anything like you. But he's sweet. He's teaching me to play chess."

"How's he feel about all this?" I said.

"He's afraid to come to school."

I nodded.

"And where do I come in?" I said. "Or are we just making conversation?"

"I told him you'd help him," Jeannie said.

Chapter 34

Jeannie and I sat with Aurelio Lopez on a bench outside a bodega in the Mexican neighborhood that everyone called Chihuahua. He was a smallish kid, slim, with longish black hair and big dark eyes. One eye was bruised and swollen half shut.

"I don't even think of myself as a Mexican," he said. "I don't wake up in the morning and think, you are Mexican, you dog. My father came up here before I was born to work in the mine. I never even been to Mexico."

I nodded.

"This stuff happen to a lot of Mexican kids or just you?" I said.

Aurelio shrugged.

"I'm small," he said. "I'm easy to pick on."

"So," I said. "How many guys are there?"

"I don't know, about ten, I guess," Aurelio said. "They pick on the girls too."

"Mexican girls?" I asked.

"Yes."

"They ever tease you?" I said to Jeannie.

"Sometimes," she said. "When I'm with Aurelio. They call me names."

"Like what?"

"Spick lover," she said. "Beaner girl."

I made a face.

"So who are these guys?" I said.

"I don't know," Aurelio said. "I don't hang with any Anglos except Jeannie."

"Well, I guess we'll probably find out," I said.

"I wish I was a tough guy," Aurelio said. "Like you, Spenser. But I'm not."

"Everybody gotta be what they are," I said.

Jeannie looked at me.

"What are you going to do?" she said.

"I can walk to and from school with you every day," I said to Aurelio. "If you want."

Aurelio nodded.

"But what are you going to do against ten guys?" he said.

"Excellent question," I said.

"Do you have an excellent answer?" Jeannie said.

"Not yet," I said.

Chapter 35

"Let me guess, you took it on," Susan said.

"Yep."

She smiled at me like a mother at an unusual child. "You never thought about speaking to the school principal?" she said.

"Oh, God, no," I said.

"Not done?" Susan said.

"Not by fourteen-year-old boys," I said. "Wouldn't have done any good anyway."

Susan nodded.

"Schools are notoriously ineffective," she said, "at the prevention of bullying."

"And most other things," I said.

"You've never been a fan of the school system," Susan said.

"True," I said. "And this was a kind of systematic racial bullying. They would have had an assembly and the principal would have told everybody not to do it."

"And all the bigots and bullies would have said, 'Oh, gee, okay,'" Susan said.

"And beat the hell out of Aurelio Lopez," I said, "as soon as class got out."

"Probably," Susan said. "How about the police?"

"Tell you the truth, I never thought of it," I said.

"No," Susan said. "Of course not. I can remember how hermetically sealed adolescence was."

"Even for well-mannered Jewish girls growing up in Swampscott?" I said.

"Even for them. Life was you and the other kids," she said. "Adults were remote."

"That's right," I said.

"So you decided to protect him," she said.

"I did."

"Fourteen years old," she said.

"Almost fifteen," I said.

She smiled.

"Oh, well, that makes it different," she said. "Were you reading *King Arthur* at the time?"

"No," I said. "But they read it to me when I was about twelve—the Thomas Malory one, as I recall. Not Tennyson."

"And you swallowed it all," Susan said.

"Yep."

"And you still do," she said.

"Yep."

"Knight-errant," she said.

"There are worse careers," I said.

The afternoon was dwindling, and the sun was at our backs. Susan smiled and patted my hand.

"Far worse," she said. "Did you have a plan?"

"Not really," I said.

"You were going to just plow along," she said, "and assume you could handle what came your way."

"Pretty much," I said.

"Like you've done all your life."

"It's worked okay so far," I said.

"Yes," she said. "Did your father and your uncles know?"

"Yes, I talked it over with them."

"Even though they were adults," Susan said.

"Not the same," I said. "There wasn't much adult-child stuff going on at my house. I was one member of a family of four. They were the other three."

"No wonder," Susan said, "you're not quite like other men."

"That a good thing?" I said.

"Yes," Susan said. "I think so."

Chapter 36

"You feel like you gotta do this," Cash said.

"Yes."

"How you gonna go about it?" Patrick said.

"I'll walk with him to school and back home and see what happens," I said.

We were in the kitchen, at the table, except my father, who was at the stove with a chicken stew.

"One thing," my father said from the stove. "No weapons."

I nodded.

"Anybody flashes a weapon, you get the hell out of there and come tell us."

I nodded.

"Your word?" my father said.

"My word," I said.

"Okay," my father said.

"Sounds like the kid's gonna be outnumbered, Sam," Cash said.

"He wanted us to help him, he'd a asked us," my father said. "He knows how to fight. He don't seem to scare easy."

"And we can't be going out and beating the hell out of fifteen-year-old kids," Patrick said.

Cash nodded.

My father brought the pot from the stove and began to serve the stew.

"And this Aurelio kid shouldn't have to fear for his life every day at school," my father said.

"No," Cash said. "He shouldn't."

We all ate some of the stew. Pearl sat close by my leg staring at my plate, just in case.

Patrick put down his fork and drank some beer from the bottle and put the beer down and wiped his mouth with his napkin.

"You won't have much trouble with one-on-one," he said, and grinned. "You been well trained."

I nodded.

"But if you gotta go up against a bunch of guys, there's some tactics to think about."

"You've all taught me how to fight more than one guy," I said. "How to punch and pivot and punch and slide. You been drilling me for years."

"That's fighting two people," Cash said. "Maybe even three."

"But with a bunch of people," Patrick said, "you gotta pick out the leader."

"And separate him from the others," Cash said.

"So it's just you and him, one-on-one," Patrick said. "Not you against ten."

I nodded. Pearl rested her head on my thigh.

"Any kind of confrontation," my father said, "you need to manage it. Don't let the other guy manage it."

"If I can," I said.

"If you can," my father said.

"And if I can't?"

"You run," my father said.

"Run?"

"Sure, running is part of managing the situation. You're outnumbered or outmanned, run, come back to it when you can manage it."

"I can't just run," I said.

My father looked at my uncles, then back at me.

"We been teaching you how to fight," my father said. "We have not been teaching you how to be a fool."

Cash and Patrick nodded. All three of them looked at me. I nodded.

"You're a tough kid," my father said. "It's probably in your bloodlines. You're going to be a tough man."

"And pretty soon," Patrick said. "You've grown up a lot since you went down the river with Jeannie."

"Where," Cash said, "you were brave enough, but you also had to run away from Luke in order to manage the situation."

"Same with the black bear," Patrick said.

It all suddenly seemed to kick in.

"Yes," I said. "That's right."

"So do what you need to do," my father said. "And know that you got a place to run to and backup if you need it."

I looked around the table at the three of them.

"Yes," I said. "I've always known that."

Chapter 37

I met Aurelio at the head of his street and walked the ten blocks to school with him. He was pale and swallowed often.

"Scared?" I said.

"They hate me," he said.

"I bet they don't," I said. "It's just that they can pick on you, so they do."

"But why?"

"Some kids are like that," I said.

"Why don't they leave other kids alone?" Aurelio said.

"I don't know," I said. "I suppose it makes them feel important."

As we reached the school yard, a kid named Turk Ferris, that I played football with, yelled, "Hey, *maricón*!"

"What's *'maricón'* mean?" I said to Aurelio.

"Pansy," he said.

Another guy I knew, Carl Dodge, said, "Hey, Spenser, how come you're walking with the little greaser?"

"Aurelio," I said.

"Okay," Carl said. "How come you're walking with Aurelio?"

"He's a friend of mine," I said.

Carl shrugged. Aurelio and I went on into the school and were in our homeroom when the bell rang. Aurelio sat up front. I sat in the back. Turk Ferris sat beside me. English was our first class. Mr. Hartley was the teacher. We were reading *A Tale of Two Cities*. Turk opened his book and pretended to be reading it while he talked to me.

"How come you're hanging around with Mexicans?" he said.

"I like Aurelio," I said.

"He's queer, man," Turk said.

"You think?" I said.

"A *maricón*," Turk said.

"That a new word you learned?" I said.

"*Maricón*," Turk said. "Aurelio *Maricón*."

"I don't know if he's queer," I said. "But if you're right, and he is, does that mean he has to get beat up every couple days?"

"How 'bout 'cause he's a beaner?" Turk said.

"Whatever," I said. "Why you want to beat him up?"

"'Cause we don't like them."

"Them?"

"Mexicans," Turk said. "You gonna protect him?"

"I'm gonna protect him," I said.

"I never had you figured for a spick lover, man."

Mr. Hartley said, "I'd like some quiet, please, in the back of the room."

We sat still, and when Mr. Hartley looked back down at his notes, I whispered to Turk, "Just leave him alone."

Mr. Hartley looked up again and saw Turk and me looking at him innocently, eager for knowledge.

Chapter 38

The low buildings of the Back Bay were dark. They looked, with the effusive sunset behind them, like a stage setting.

Standing on the little bridge, Susan and I turned and rested our hips on the bridge bulwark and looked at it.

"That's very pretty," Susan said.

"And it happens every day," I said.

"I've heard that," Susan said. "Was Aurelio really gay?"

"Don't know," I said.

"You didn't ask him?"

"No," I said.

"You didn't care," Susan said.

"No," I said. "Didn't then and don't now."

"Mexican either," Susan said.

"Nope," I said. "Mexican either. I never cared about that stuff."

I grinned at her.

"Besides, I was a little hazy on exactly what it meant to be gay," I said.

"Did they keep bothering you?" Susan said.

"Not bad, for a while. They teased us a little, but I didn't have to fight anybody."

"Were they scared of you?"

"Maybe a little scared," I said. "They knew I could fight. But, you know, I played ball with a lot of the guys. I knew most of them. They all knew I'd punched out Croy Davis, who was two years older than I was. And I kept telling them to lay off Aurelio."

"And they listened?"

"Some," I said.

"So you were able to stop walking to school with him after a while."

"I was, until a bunch of Mexican kids beat the crap out of an Anglo kid and everybody started taking sides."

"Which, unless you were more different in those days than I think you were, wasn't your style."

"No, it wasn't," I said.

"You've never been a joiner," Susan said.

"I wasn't trying to solve race relations in town," I said. "I was just trying to help Aurelio, because he was a nice little guy and because Jeannie asked me to."

"When I was at Harvard," Susan said, "the concern was mostly with larger problems, saving the world, that kind of thing."

"How's that working?" I said.

Susan smiled.

"Since I've known you," she said, "you have actually been saving the world, one person at a time."

I grinned.

"I guess I work on a smaller scale than Harvard," I said.

"Thank God," Susan said.

Chapter 39

I was leaning against the brick wall on the sunny side of the school, talking to Jeannie and Aurelio at recess. Carl and Turk came over to us along with an older guy I didn't know. All three of them looked hard at Aurelio. But nobody spoke to him. I could feel Aurelio trying to shrink into the brick wall.

"How ya doin', Spenser?" Carl said.

"Good," I said.

"Hey, babe," Turk said.

Jeannie ignored him.

"This here is Leo Roemer," Carl said.

"Leo," I said.

He nodded. He looked at Jeannie.

"Who's this?" he said.

"I'm Jeannie," she said.

Leo nodded.

"Not bad," he said.

"Gee, thanks," Jeannie said. "You're pretty cute yourself."

"Maybe someday I'll show you how cute I am," Leo said.

"Maybe," Jeannie said. "Maybe not."

"You go to school here?" I said.

"I don't go to school nowhere," Leo said. "I dumped it after the eighth grade."

"Lucky you," I said.

"It's all crap anyway," he said.

I nodded.

"Leo's gonna help us with the spicks," Carl said.

I nodded.

"And we gotta know where you stand," Carl said.

"Stand about what?" I said.

"You with us against the spicks or you with them?" Turk said.

"I'm just looking out for Aurelio," I said.

"They beat up Sal Dusack," Turk said.

"Probably getting even," I said.

"Hey," Leo said. "You with us or not?"

"Whaddya do, Leo?" I said. "Now that you're not in school."

"I work with my old man," he said.

"What did you say your last name was?"

"Roemer," he said. "What do you care?"

"Roemer Construction?"

"Yeah, whaddya know about it?"

"My father is Sam Spenser," I said. "He and my uncles do a lot of work with your father."

"Yeah? Well, I don't care," Leo said. "I want to know where you stand."

"You know any of them?" I said.

"I don't work with the subcontractors," Leo said. "You with us or against us?"

"How about neither?" I said.

"We don't like 'neither,'" Leo said.

He looked around at Carl and Turk.

"Do we?" he said.

"No," Carl said.

"Come on, Spenser," Turk said. "You known us all your life."

"How can you side with them?" Carl said.

"I'm not siding with them," I said. "And I'm not siding with you."

"You're American," Turk said. "Like us."

"I might not be exactly like you," I said.

"Aw, screw him," Leo said to Carl and Turk. "He's yellow. He won't even fight for his own kind."

My father always said there was no point in arguing about crap; when you got all through, the argument was still gonna be crap.

I made no comment.

The three of them turned away.

"Better watch yourself, Spenser," Leo said.

Turk looked back at me and shook his head. I shrugged at him. And they walked off.

Chapter 40

"What's going to happen?" Aurelio said.

"Don't know," I said.

"I think there's going to be a big fight," Jeannie said.

"Do you think so?" Aurelio said to me.

"I don't know," I said.

"I don't like that Leo," Jeannie said.

"What's going to happen?" Aurelio asked. "If everybody starts fighting, you can't protect me from all of them."

"They might not be so interested in you alone," I said.

"But you'll stay with me?" Aurelio said.

"Yes."

"I don't like that Leo," Jeannie said again.

"No," I said. "I don't like him either."

"How old do you think he is?" Jeannie said.

"Sixteen," I said. "Seventeen."

"You think he really works for his father?" Jeannie said.

"He didn't know my father and my uncles. If he did much in the business, he'd know them. They do a lot of work for Roemer."

"I bet he just hangs around the office," Jeannie said.

"Could be," I said.

"I'm scared about all this," Jeannie said.

"I don't like it much either," I said.

"Are you scared?" Aurelio said.

"Some," I said.

"But you'll stick with me?" Aurelio said.

"I will."

"What are you scared of most?" Jeannie asked me.

"It's gotten awful big," I said. "And . . . I never had a fight with a guy sixteen, seventeen years old. That's a pretty big difference."

"Maybe you won't have to fight with him," Jeannie said.

"Maybe," I said.

"But you think you will," Jeannie said.

"Yes."

"Why?" she said.

"Because he didn't scare me," I said. "At least not that he could tell."

"So?"

"So he was supposed to, I mean, it's why he came over. The guys wanted me with them, and I wouldn't do it, so they bring in big bad Leo, and I still won't do it."

"But," Jeannie said, "I should think if you weren't scared of him, he'd less want to fight you, you know?"

"Guy like Leo, there's a reason he hangs around with younger guys," I said. "Maybe the guys his age don't think he's such a big deal."

"Like the guys at the construction company?" Jeannie said.

"Maybe," I said. "Maybe he needs to be a tough guy and they won't treat him like one."

"That doesn't make any sense to me," Jeannie said. "Is it because I'm a girl?"

She looked at Aurelio.

"Does that make any sense to you, Aurelio?" she said.

He shook his head slowly.

"No, but I know a lot of boys need to be macho," he said.

"Are you like that?" Jeannie asked me.

"I suppose," I said. "Some."

"But you don't pick on people," Jeannie said.

"No," I said. "It doesn't make me feel brave."

"Is that what it's about?" Jeannie said. "Feeling brave?"

"Maybe," I said. "But you can only feel brave if you face up to something that you need to be brave about, you know?"

"Like with my father?"

"Yes."

"And like trying to protect Aurelio," she said.

"Yes."

Jeannie shook her head.

"You are not like any other boy I know," she said.

"I was brought up a little different, I guess."

"Because you didn't have a mother?" Jeannie said.

"I don't know. I never had a mother; I don't

know what that would be like. But being brought up by my father and my uncles, the way they treated me."

"Which is how?" Jeannie said.

"Like I wasn't a kid," I said. "Like I was a person."

"And they're all brave," Jeannie said.

"They are," I said.

"Is it so important feeling brave?" Jeannie said.

"I guess it is," I said.

"God," Jeannie said. "Being a boy must not be easy."

"No," I said. "No easier than being a girl."

"Being a kid," Aurelio said, "is especially not easy."

Chapter 41

A kid named Petey Hernandez stopped me in the corridor when school was letting out. He was fifteen and already had a scar on his left forearm where someone had cut him with a knife.

"Got a minute?" he said.

I said I did.

"We know how you been looking out for Aurelio Lopez," he said.

I nodded.

"Aurelio ain't much," Petey said. "But he's Mexican, and I figure we owe you for it."

"You don't owe me anything," I said.

Petey shrugged.

"Anyway," he said, "Aurelio ain't the only Mexican they been beatin' on."

"Who's 'they'?" I said.

"Roemer and his pack," Petey said.

I nodded. Croy went by us without making eye contact.

"How 'bout Croy?" I said. "He in the pack?"

"Yeah," Petey said. "Wouldn't you figure?"

"Seems the type," I said.

Petey nodded.

"Gonna be a rumble," he said.

"Yeah?"

"Down back of the Y," Petey said. "Roemer and his buddies like to hang out there. We gonna go down there and settle things."

"When?" I said.

Petey shook his head.

"You don't need to know," he said.

"Why you telling me at all?" I said.

"So you'll stay away from those guys," he said. "Don't want to see you get hurt."

I nodded.

"I don't hang with them," I said.

"Good idea," Petey said. "You gonna tell anyone about this?"

"Nobody you'd care about," I said.

"Nobody at all," Petey said.

"Might talk about it with my father and my

uncles. They won't say anything if I ask them not to."

"You can trust them?"

"Certain sure," I said.

"You gimme your word?" he said.

"It ain't about me," I said.

"Your word?" he said. "Nobody tells Roemer?"

I nodded.

"My word."

"I think your word's good," Petey said. "It ain't, you'll hear from us."

"It ain't my fight," I said. "I got nothing to say about it."

"Make sure," Petey said.

"I'll do what I can," I said.

Petey nodded and turned and walked away. I watched him go.

Tough kid, I thought. Lot tougher than Leo Roemer.

Chapter 42

"Sun's down," Susan said. "And it's getting chilly. I think we should go across the street and have a glass of wine at The Bristol Lounge."

"What a good idea," I said.

We walked off the little bridge and headed past the last of the cruising swan boats toward Boylston Street.

Susan took my hand as we walked.

"Was that Mexican boy's name really Petey?" she said.

"Pedro," I said.

"Did they fight?" she said.

I smiled.

"Yep," I said.

"And?" Susan said.

"The Anglos got outthought," I said. "The Mexicans sent one of their smallest guys down back of the Y. He let Roemer and his group see him, and he fired an apple at them and ran. Of course they chased him. He ran across the street to the Public Works parking lot, full of trucks and plows and tractors, and hid in there. Leo Roemer and his troop come after him and start looking for him, which causes them to split up into small groups looking in and around the heavy equipment, which is parked in rows with an aisle in between. The Mexican kids are in there waiting. When the Anglos get in among the trucks, Petey's boys jump them, and, because the Anglos are split up, they are always outnumbered by the Mexican kids, and they get their tails whipped. The fight ends with Leo, with a bloody nose, leading his troop out of there at a dead run."

"And you think Petey planned this out before it happened?" Susan said.

"Down to the apple," I said. "If it was a stone or something that would do damage, they might have been scared to chase him into the lot. But an apple doesn't scare anybody, just annoys them."

"And he knew when they got to the lot, they'd

split up and start looking up and down the aisles."

I nodded.

"And how do you know about this?" she said. "Did you attend?"

"No," I said. "Aurelio told me."

"Did he attend?"

"Nope, but some of the other Mexican kids told him about it," I said. "And pretty much it was all over town by the next afternoon . . ." I grinned at the memory. "And Leo was seen around town with a black eye and a fat lip."

"You seem glad the Mexican boys won."

"I didn't care who won," I said. "I never got that whole business about racial loyalty, or gender loyalty, or age loyalty. I always, even when I was little, tried to take things as they came and like or dislike them on how they were."

"You still do," Susan said.

"Yes," I said. "But even now I still kind of admire how smart Pedro was. Gang for gang, I think he was outnumbered."

We went into the Four Seasons hotel. Both

doormen spoke warmly to Susan. We walked to the lounge in silence and got a seat at the bar. Susan ordered a glass of pinot grigio. I had a beer.

"Was that the end of it?" Susan said.

"Not quite," I said.

Chapter 43

It was overcast and kind of cold, and there was no one else in the school yard. I was working on my jump shot, with Jeannie retrieving the ball for me. Catch the pass, take a dribble, square up, shoot. Catch the pass, take a dribble, square up, shoot. Jeannie's passes were not always really good, but it was better than chasing it after every shot. I was good with the dribble. I could pass, and I was tough on defense. But my outside shot was weak and so I tried to do a hundred jumpers every day.

I was on number sixty-seven when Leo and his troop came around the corner of the school. Croy was beside Leo.

Leo shouted at me, "You're in trouble now, Spenser."

I sank jumper number sixty-eight before I looked at him. Jeannie retrieved the ball and held it for a moment, then she dropped the basketball and ran away. Leo watched her go and turned and looked at me.

"Smart girl," he said.

"What's your problem, Leo?" I said.

"You knew the Mexicans was gonna ambush us, and you didn't tell us," Leo shouted.

"Nope," I said.

"Don't lie about it," Leo yelled. "Croy seen you talking to Petey Hernandez right before the fight. You betrayed your own damn kind."

"You are my kind?" I said. "I don't think so."

"You admit you knew it?" Leo said.

"Nothing to admit," I said. "I didn't know what they were planning."

Leo and his gang moved closer. I noticed Croy stuck pretty close to Leo.

"You think you can fight us all?" Leo said.

Besides him and Croy there were about ten other kids. The answer was obviously *no*. But I didn't care to say so.

"You ready to get it handed to you, backstabber?" Leo said.

"You first?" I said.

"All of us first," Leo said.

The gang spread out and formed a circle around me. They didn't seem in any hurry. I think they wanted me to be scared. I was scared. But I did everything I could to keep them from seeing it. I kept facing Leo, the leader. And as the circle formed, I took a step closer to him.

I said, "You and me, Leo? One-on-one?"

"Why should I do that?" Leo said. "There's twelve of us. Why should I do all the work?"

Everyone was quiet. It felt thick and strained, like it does just before a storm breaks. I was debating whether to hit Leo first. I had just decided to hit him when my father's gray pickup truck pulled into the school yard and my father and my two uncles got out. I felt all the tightness go out of my stomach. My back loosened. My breathing slowed a little. My father and my uncles pushed through the circle of boys as if they weren't there, and walked to where I was, and stood in a semicircle behind me.

Nobody said anything.

Finally Leo said to my father, "This is just us kids fooling around, Mr. Spenser."

"Lot of you," my father said. "Just thought there should be a few more with him."

"What are you gonna do?" Leo said.

My father ignored him.

"You think you're gonna have to fight him?" my father said to me.

"Yes," I said.

"Now's a good time, then," my father said.

"Oh, sure," Leo said. "And when I kick his butt, you big guys jump me?"

"Nope," my father said.

"What'll you do?" Leo said.

"Can't handle losing," my father said, "you got no business fighting."

"You touch me and my father will sue your ass," Leo said.

My father smiled faintly.

"You two fight," he said, "we'll see that it's fair, and win or lose, when it's over it's over and everybody goes home."

"Okay, Leo?" I said. "You and me?"

He didn't answer. I slid into the fighting stance they had spent so long teaching me.

"Don't rush things," Patrick said to me.

Leo tried to kick me in the groin, but I turned my hip and put a jab on his nose. The nose had recently taken a beating thanks to Petey and his friends. It was tender. He yelped. I followed with a right cross. He backed up. I shuffled after him. He hit me with a big looping right hand, which I half blocked. He followed that with an equally looping left, which I stepped inside of, blocked with both forearms and slammed him on the side of the head with a back fist. He tried to get his arms around me. I drove both my hands, palms up, under his chin and bent his head back and shoved him away. He tried once more and I hit him with a flurry of lefts and rights. He put his hands up to protect his head and I started hooking him in the ribs, left, right, driving off my legs, out of a crouch like they had taught me.

He quit.

He put both hands against the back of his head, and shielded his face with his forearms, and doubled up and dropped to his knees. I thought about kicking him. My heart was pumping, my breath was hard but steady, I could feel the rhythm of the fight in my whole self. I shook my head. Instead I looked around at the circle of boys.

"Anybody else?" I said.

Nobody met my eyes. As I surveyed the circle, I saw Jeannie behind it, near my father's truck.

"She come get you?" I said to my father.

"She did," he said.

I looked around the circle again. Then I looked at Leo, still crouched on the ground.

"Over," I said.

With his hand still clasped to his head, Leo nodded.

"You need a ride home?" my father said to Leo.

Leo shook his head.

"Your old man has anything he wants to discuss with me," my father said, "or Cash or Patrick, he knows where we live."

Leo shook his head again. My father stared down at him.

"You're not going to tell him, are you?" my father asked.

With his head still protected, looking at the ground, Leo said, "No."

"Why not?" my father said.

"He'd yell at me for losing," Leo said.

My father reached down and took hold of Leo's arm and helped him stand.

"He's wrong to do that," my father said. "Everybody loses sometime. You ever need to talk, come see me."

Leo nodded.

My uncle Cash looked at the circle of kids still standing around uneasily.

"Time to go home," Cash said.

Nobody moved for a moment.

"Now," Cash said. "Right now."

The kids sort of came awake and turned and went off in various directions.

Jeannie came over.

"I'll walk you home," she said to Leo.

I said, "Thanks, Jeannie."

She nodded and patted my shoulder. Then she took Leo's arm and led him toward home.

"She feels sorry for him," Patrick said.

"I do too," I said.

"Not bad enough to let him beat you," Patrick said.

"No," I said. "Not that bad."

Chapter 44

My uncle Cash put out a pan of ice water and told me to soak my hands.

"Otherwise they'll swell up," he said.

My father sat opposite me at the kitchen table.

"Keep your hands in there, long as you can," he said. "Then take 'em out, let 'em rest and put 'em back in. Goal is twenty minutes or so."

I nodded.

"Jeannie came and got you," I said.

"Yep."

"What did she say?"

"Told us there was a bunch of kids gonna hurt you," my father said. "I asked her how many. She said twenty."

"Twelve," I said.

"You counted," my father said.

"Yes."

My father nodded once like that was a good thing to have done. I took my hands out of the ice water. They were numb with cold.

"Put your hands back in as soon as you can," my father said.

"Jeannie's a good kid," I said.

"She is," my father said.

"She wants me to be her boyfriend," I said.

My father nodded.

"You want that?"

"No," I said. "I don't. I like her, but I don't like her that way."

"Can't love somebody just because they want you to," my father said.

"Dad," I said. "I'm only fifteen."

"I loved your mother," my father said. "When I was fifteen. Probably loved her when I was five."

I nodded.

"I feel bad for her, though," I said.

"That's not enough," Cash said.

"Don't do her any favors," Patrick said. "You let her think you love her, and in a while she'll know you don't, and you won't be enough."

"So I'd be hurting her by trying not to hurt her," I said.

"If what she feels for you is real," my father said.

"That's weird," I said.

Patrick grinned at me.

"That's life," he said.

"Life's not simple," I said.

"No," my father said. "And not every problem has a happy solution. You don't need to soak your hands anymore."

I removed my hands, picked up the bucket and dumped the water in the kitchen sink.

"You three guys always seem to know what to do," I said.

"We've lived awhile," my father said.

"Lot of people have lived awhile," I said. "How come you guys know all this stuff?"

The three of them looked at each other as if they'd never thought about it.

Finally my father said, "We pay attention."

Chapter 45

"**You** were still looking for the one?" Susan said.

"I guess," I said.

"You ever wonder why you have been so dogged to that commitment?" Susan said.

"Looking for you," I said.

"Looking for someone," she said, "like looking for a pattern, and when we met, I fit the pattern nicely."

"A less romantic explanation," I said.

"But one rooted at least in possibility."

"A pox on all your science," I said.

"So where did the pattern come from?" Susan said.

"That I was looking for, that you fit nicely into?" I said.

"That one."

"Well, first of all," I said, "I'm willing to accept

the fact that I could have met someone else and loved them. But I stick to my guns on a simple fact."

I sipped my drink.

"Which is?" Susan said.

"You were the one."

"The one you imagined," Susan said.

"Yes."

"So," she said, "quite literally the girl of your dreams, as you like to say."

"Yes."

"Do you know why you were so committed to the one?" Susan said.

I smiled at her.

"Yes," I said. "I believe I do."

Susan looked at me and raised her eyebrows and cocked her head.

"I grew up in an all-male family," I said. "A good family, but one without a woman in it. I think I was always trying to complete the family."

"Which I did," Susan said.

"Yes."

"So you knew that all along," Susan said.

"I figured it out after I met you," I said.

"How did that make you feel?" Susan said.

"Maybe I was looking for a missing mother," I said. "The fact remains that out of all the women I have known, you were the only one I loved."

"And I loved you back," Susan said.

"So even though you're a Harvard PhD shrink," I said, "you still believe in love."

"Yes," she said. "I've overcome my education."

"Atta girl," I said.

Chapter 46

Looking back, it was like a Norman Rockwell painting. My father and my two uncles and me at the train station. I had made all state in football my senior year and gotten some scholarship offers. My father had urged me to take the one in Boston because he still thought Boston was the intellectual hub of the universe. He hadn't made me choose Boston, but he urged as strong as I had ever heard him. So, I went to Boston.

"You get to Denver," my father said. "You take a cab to Denver Airport and stay in this motel. In the morning you go to the terminal and check in and fly to Boston. It's all right here on this ticket envelope. Be about four hours or so. You take a cab to the college and do what they tell you. Here's some money."

It was a pretty good wad of cash.

"Can you afford this?" I said.

"Three of us working," Cash said.

"And we don't need much," Patrick said.

"Open a bank account, like I told you," my father said. "Put the money in it. We can wire you more when you need it."

The train to Denver started to board.

"Okay," I said.

I hugged each of them. I could feel my eyes begin to tear.

"Okay," I said again.

I picked up my suitcase and stood for a moment looking at them. *My God!* They were tearing up too.

"Take care of yourself," Cash said.

Patrick nodded without speaking.

"We're here," my father said.

I nodded and made a small hand wave at them and stepped up into the train. I found an empty seat by the window and looked out it and cried as the train pulled out of the station.

Chapter 47

"I wished they could come with me," I said.

"You were never away before," Susan said.

"Except for my trip down the river with Jeannie," I said.

"Of course you were homesick. How did college go?"

"I played strong safety," I said. "And returned punts. At the start of my junior year, I tore up my knee and couldn't play anymore."

"And you didn't stay in college?"

"No," I said. "Without a scholarship we couldn't afford it. So I quit and boxed for a while."

"You were good?"

"I was good, and I got a lot of fights. The Great White Hope and a former college kid to boot."

"But you didn't like it," she said.

"I fought a couple guys who became contenders, one became champ for a while. And I realized the difference. I was good. They were great. And the only way I was going to get to the top was to play the White College Boy thing."

"Which you didn't want to do," Susan said.

"Correct," I said. "So I moved on and took the exam and got on the state cops and you know how that all went."

"And you weren't tempted to go back to West Flub-a-dub?" Susan said.

"My father and I talked about that," I said. "He was certain that Boston was where I should be and I was too. So I stayed and missed them every day."

"They were here," Susan said.

I looked at her for a moment.

"They are here now," she said. "With us. Wherever you are, they will be. You contain them."

I felt my throat tighten for a moment. I nodded slowly.

"Yes," I said. "With us."